The P-Town Queen

Other Books By Annie Hoff

Georgette Alden Starts Over

Deslisle Publications

The P-Town Queen

By

Annie Hoff

**CLIMAX, SK
CANADA**

This is a work of fiction. The characters, incidents and dialogues in this book are of the author's imagination and are not to be construed as real. Any resemblance to actual events or persons, living or dead, is completely coincidental.

No part of this book may be reproduced or transmitted in any form or by any means, electronic or mechanical, including photocopying, recording, or by any information storage and retrieval system, without permission in writing from the publisher.

Copyright 2019 by Annie Hoff
December 2019
ISBN 978-1-989276-13-6
Cover Art by Petra's Art
Produced in Canada

Dedication

To Jim, who first showed me Cape Cod.

Acknowledgements

It might not take a village to write a book, but it surely does take a whole town to get that book up and ready for publication.

Thanks to Deborah Jelley, Sherry Steffensmeyer, Carolyn Saari, Suzanne Ahmad, Kathy Pile, Alex Hayes, Fran LeMoine, Tammy McCracken, Teresa Jones, Kate Johnson, Harriet Reindeaux, Kim Brady, and Suzanne Shriver, who listened and read as I struggled through early drafts.

And a special shout out to J. Ellen Smith, who gave this book a chance and to my partner in crime, Diane Badzinsky, whose diligent edits polished all my words.

Chapter One

Nikki

I did not blow up the *Mona Lisa*. Not only did I not blow up the *Mona Lisa*—an old leaker of a boat whose blowing up could be construed as a favor to the aptly named Rusty Cook—I did not blow up any part of Rusty's marina. My brothers will, of course, say otherwise. They had quite the laugh at my expense over coffee at Ella's Place.

Rusty had been on the lookout for a boat for me. It had taken a lot of gumption and crow-eating to get to a place where I could consider buying a boat. I needed a cheap one, because God only knew how much money I'd be able to squeeze out of the Massachusetts Bay Commission via the research grant proposal I'd spent three long months laboring to produce.

The head of the commission was Ned Anderson. Ned, a brilliant shark researcher in his own right, had tumbled a long way: to full time administrator of a bullshit state commission. Though to hear Ned say it, it wasn't a tumble but a reward for all the years he'd spent roughing it on a California channel island—an island that only had electricity every other day— in order to unlock the mystery of white shark feeding behavior. I had spent five years on that island with Ned. We were married at the time.

One divorce and one un-granted California grant later, I was back on Cape Cod, in Provincetown, living just off Bradford Street with my father and in dire need of a job. I wrote the proposal. Then I revved up my resolve, packed away my pride, and called Ned. He agreed to a meeting at the Long Wharf Marriott in Boston. It wasn't supposed to get personal. Really. I had every intention of sticking to business.

I had my only dress dry-cleaned. I put my hair up and put on my gray suede shoes. My pop actually looked up from the TV.

"Where you off to, all done up?"

"Job interview."

"No kidding? Max Groper hiring you on?"

Max Groper was head of Coastal Studies here in Provincetown. I had asked Max for a job when I first got home, but Coastal is a small budget operation with limited funds for another researcher. The only other jobs around were fishing, which two of my brothers did, and working at Dairy Queen, which my baby brother was just shy of doing. As was I, come to think of it.

"The Bay Commission," I said, as breezily as I could manage.

"Ned's commission?" My father raised his eyebrows. I must say, he looked as though he didn't quite believe it

"It's a job, not a reconciliation," I said, not quite sure I believed it myself.

Ned and I met in the bar of the Marriot. He'd already ordered a glass of Pinot for me, knowing that would be what I wanted. The sad truth is that was what I wanted. I hated that he knew me as well as he did.

"You look great," said Ned, handing me the wine. I wish he'd said something snide, like 'your hair looks better down' or 'you've got poppy seeds in your teeth.' Either of those would have unleashed a little fury, which might have led to him wearing the Pinot instead of me drinking it. Then again, that wouldn't have gotten me anywhere. Not that I got anywhere except to a room on the fifth floor.

I'm not proud of myself and it pains me to even mention it. All that I can offer in my defense is that Ned is six four, blond, and was probably a Viking in a former life. He looked good in a suit. We had a fairly passionate history, a history I could not easily forget, and after half an hour and two wines, it felt as though we'd never left that island. One thing led to another. Ned said something to the effect of 'I've missed you,' and I said something likewise, which led to hand holding and a little light kissing. Then Ned said that he thought about us a lot and recounted those nights without electricity when we'd found other ways to stay warm and he said he missed those nights. And I said I missed them too and thus the whole train wreck was set into motion.

We got a room, consensually. And

everything that happened in said room was entirely consensual. It felt familiar, right down to Ned's hogging the blankets and me having to tug them back in the middle of the night. All that familiarity led to regret. By 5:00 a.m., after spending a sleepless hour watching Ned's chest rise and fall under the bedspread, I was ready to admit that everything that had come between us was my fault. I put my hand to his shoulder and he stirred. "Ned?"

"What?" he opened his eyes, looking groggy and unsure of where he was. "What time is it?"

"We need to talk."

Ned leaned up on an elbow to eye the clock radio next to the supersized bed. "Oh God. I've got to go."

"Go? What about...?" I'd been ready to pour my heart out like a packet of Splenda.

Ned was already out of bed, hunting for pants and socks, swearing to himself. He handed me a menu. "Order up room service. They have fresh fruit. Get whatever you like. Bill it to the room."

I handed the menu back. Actually, I threw it at him. He ducked and it thudded against the wall. "I don't need to be compensated."

"I'd like to stay, babe, but I've really got to go. I'll talk to Senator McGowan. I'll set up a meeting. I promise."

I stared at him as he re-tied his tie. I wish I'd thought of a comeback, but I was too stunned. "So slam, bam, thank you, ma'am," I managed.

He turned around. "Nik, don't. Okay?"

Then he gathered up his briefcase. And, upon walking out the door, actually said, "I'll call you."

So there you have it, five years on an island with sporadic electricity and you get breakfast and I'll call you. He did call. Guilt or regret had gotten the ball rolling. Senator McGowan was itching to visit the Cape in April and we could talk about a grant. On the night before my big meeting with the senator and Ned, Rusty called to say he'd found the perfect vessel for my research. A beautiful sparkler of a morning that promised spring also seemed to portend a bright future as Rusty and I climbed aboard the *Mona Lisa*. Rusty pulled the throttle and morning birdsong gave way to the cough and rumble of an engine. Dark clouds scattered to the horizon and perfumed the air with motor oil.

"She's a little rusty," Rusty said, chuckling at his pun. "but she's ship shape, don't you worry about that."

I all but rolled my eyes at him. My brothers were fishermen, my father and uncle had been fishermen, and my grandfathers, both of them, had been fishermen. In short, I came from a long line of fisher folk and I knew from boats. I would have bet my Portuguese American ass that the *Mona Lisa* was hardly ship shape. "Does she come with a bailing bucket?" I asked Rusty.

Rusty chuckled again. "She's a good boat. A good boat," he said, petting the wheel as though she might be asked to go fetch.

"Did Leonardo da Vinci christen her himself?" I asked, scraping a flake of rust from her side.

"That's good. Funny. No. How about we go below deck? I'll show you the galley," Rusty said, nearly running for the ancient stairs that led to the ship's aptly named bowels. Below deck the *Mona Lisa* smelled as though she hadn't been aired since she was built some fifty years earlier. Rusty, seemingly oblivious to the overpowering mildew, put a pudgy hand to the two-burner stove wedged into a dark corner. "The stove's near new," he said, running his hand, which still bore his Provincetown High class ring, along the burner's rim. The hand landed on the control knob and he turned the gas, which didn't light the gas ring. He tried again, still nothing but a mild gassy odor accompanied by a strange hum that rose from the stove well.

For a minute I wondered if mildew could make a sound. Though if it could, I imagined it would be more like the hiss of a snake than a hum or a buzz. This noise had a definite buzzing quality. The pudgy class-ringed hand that Rusty had been using to turn the burner knob off and on and off and on came up and swatted its owner on the ear. And in another half minute the buzzing materialized into a swarm of bees. Bees angry at being disturbed after long months of peace in the bowels of the *Mona Lisa*.

I grabbed the stair rail and chugged up the stairs, Rusty and the bees tight on my heels. And, although I was not inclined to swim the Atlantic in April, I hoisted myself over the boat's side into the icy water. Rusty cannonballed in beside me, causing a wave that set the water around the *Mona* into a tizzy.

We climbed onto the dock looking like half-drowned seals. I'd worn the same dress and suede pumps that had so impressed Ned a month earlier. The pumps had changed from soft gray to ruined wet.

"The bees are no problem," Rusty brushed down his chinos as though taking a dive into the North Atlantic fully dressed was something he did routinely. "We can fumigate. That's all it will take. A little call to the exterminator and she'll be right as rain. Important thing is she's tight. She's one seaworthy boat."

Rusty's impromptu sales pitch was followed by a pop, which was followed by a hiss, which was followed by an earth-shattering boom. Rusty and I were hurled back into the water by the percussion. The tsunami in the explosive wake lifted us, flung us onto the beach, and left us there like flotsam. What was left of the *Mona Lisa* was floating in bits and pieces on the waves, as was what was left of the dock and the *Mona's* neighbors.

Ears ringing like the bells in the steeple of Notre Dame, Rusty and I were left dazed and numbed by the icy water, each looking to the other for proof that we had survived.

"That will solve the bee problem?" my brother Pete said over coffee at Ella's Place the next day. "Please don't tell me you actually said that to

Rusty."

I told him again that I did not blow up the boat. As to the comment, I take the Fifth.

Chapter Two

Marco

I'll never make gnocchi again. Don't get me wrong, I like a nice gnocchi and I do it up pretty good, if I do say so myself. With just the right balance of cream and garlic, it's food for the angels as my Nona would have said. But some foods, they have memories attached, and gnocchi, that's a memory I'd just as soon forget.

It was me and Angelo Del Rossi in the kitchen at Roma's. Angie, he's this big slow thug of a guy. Jesus and Mary, he didn't know a paring knife from a carving knife and was not likely to learn anytime soon. I was cooking for my silent partner, Fat Phil Lazario. Fat Phil would have owned the place outright if he didn't need somebody who knew what was what in the kitchen. Fat Phil was also my father-in-law, being as I had been married to his daughter, Lark, for a few months. Only, by then, things with Lark and me weren't so good and the week before all this happened, I'd moved out of the apartment. Lark wasn't about to tell her old man that I was living in the storage room on account of the fact that she had lied and cheated. But I got to thinking that if I came clean, Phil would recognize my value and see that Roma's could be a real jewel in downtown Newark, an up and coming area, and he'd keep his end of the bargain we'd struck and finance the place until I could buy it outright. Truth was that he'd probably keep up his end because then he could continue meeting with questionable people about questionable business propositions about which I would plead ignorance. Which was my end of the bargain. I just hoped, that after hearing my side of the story about what happened between me and Lark, Phil would think twice about meeting with some questionable guy about ending our partnership on a permanent basis.

The gnocchi had to be perfect. "What do I know from perfect?" asked Angie as I handed him the slotted spoon.

"Just taste," I said.

"Jesus, Mary, and Joe," said Angie "that's hot. What's with you, anyways?"

"I'm telling Phil that me and Lark are done for."

"Jesus, Mary, and Joe, why you want to go and do a such thing?"

Angie knew I'd caught her cheating and said he wasn't surprised being as Lark had always been a hot potato. Still, I wasn't about to tell anybody, especially not Angelo, that it wasn't one guy but three that I caught her with. It was too humiliating to think about and, to tell the truth, I didn't know what I was going to say to Phil. I hadn't really thought about what was what besides the gnocchi, which I made because it was what Phil's sainted mother always made and was probably still making up in heaven. I filled two plates with steaming pasta and ladled on my special garlic sauce and threw on just enough parmesan to make it pretty.

The dining room at Roma's had only five tables and five booths with red plastic checkered cloths and Chianti-bottle candles. The walls were paneled and the whole thing looked like the inside of a cigar box. But all I had to do was close my eyes and I could see it, the way it would be someday. Someday there'd be a plush carpet to replace the shabby green indoor-outdoor. Someday I'd have real table cloths on all the tables and strolling musicians playing requests and a wine list from here to California. If only I hadn't caught Lark in a four-way with three guys from Fat Phil's construction company.

That night the place was empty, which is where me and Phil differed in our business plan. He liked it that way and I didn't. It was empty, excepting the one booth where Phil sat across from Vladimir Dostovic, known in North Jersey as Vlad the Impaler and not because he loved his history. I should have known that Vlad and Phil sitting across from each other was suspect. They weren't, you might say, on the same side of things. Rivals might be a nice way to put it. Adversaries, if you are so inclined.

I brought the gnocchi to the table, one plate in each of my two hands. Then, just as I put the plates down, Phil drew a gun from out of nowhere and the next I knew, Vlad's head was in the gnocchi. Fat Phil looked at me with a pair of snake eyes that would scare anybody into nightmares, and my heart started to beat so hard I figured it would be coming out of my eyeballs soon.

"Have a seat," said Phil. I heard a chair scrape behind me, though I was so scared I swear to God I couldn't have turned my head if I'd wanted to. I felt Angie's big hand on my shoulder and he was pushing me down into the chair he'd brought up to the table.

Phil shoveled a forkful of pasta into his mouth. "This is good," he said, then he took a sip of Chianti to wash it down. Jesus and Joe, you'd of thought we were having a friendly conversation. Except that there was a dead guy with his head bleeding into the gnocchi across from Phil.

Phil looked up from his eats and watched me stare at the body before taking another bite of pasta. "So, what's this I hear about you and Lark?"

"I'm sorry," I said. My throat felt like it was swollen and it was hard to even squeeze those few words out. I was kind of surprised Lark had told him.

"You're sorry," Phil looked at me like he was sad about this. "Well, isn't that something? It's too fucking bad, you know. You're one hell of cook. You go behind my back, get my only daughter, my little girl, involved in Vlad's escort business. But you're fucking sorry. You think this Russian scumbag was going to do better by you than family?" Phil pointed his fork at the body. "This what you had in mind when you made deals with the competition? I treated you like my own son. But, hell, you're sorry."

I had no idea what he was talking about. "I didn't..." I started to say.

"Save your breath," Phil said. "I heard enough. I heard plenty." I felt Angie's big hand on my shoulder again. Swear to God, I'd forgotten he was there. "Get him out of here," Phil said to Angie.

"Come on," Angie picked me up by the collar. "We're going for a little ride, you and me."

My next thought, as Angie escorted me to the parking lot was that this couldn't be happening. I was just a chef from Jersey who wanted his own little restaurant. How did I all of a sudden end up in the sequel to *Goodfellas*?

Chapter Three

Nikki

By the time the police had sorted the details and the emergency first responders were assured that Rusty and I were unscathed, it was so late that I figured I'd missed the meeting. I took a hard look at myself in the rear-view of my Toyota truck. My hair stuck in waves against the side of my head like a pair of floppy ears. You could have mistaken me for a Brittany spaniel that had rolled in wet sand.

It's a testament to my desperation that I drove to the Provincetown Inn anyway. Ned's car was still in the parking lot. My first stop was the bathroom, where I attempted, with mixed results, to dry my hair under the hand dryer while using my fingers to comb out the sand. I did manage to go from looking as though I had frolicked on the beach to looking as though I'd merely lain down in a sand dune, but I would be hard pressed to say that I was anything near what would be called presentable.

Ned was sitting with a well-dressed gray-haired woman. Ned, who was facing the door, caught sight of me, said something to the woman — who I knew from photos to be the senator—and walked double pace to the door. He caught my arm and steered me into the hallway. "Where the hell have you been?"

"And a good morning to you, too."

Ned took a step back and assessed, "And what the hell happened to you?"

"A little accident. At the marina."

Ned's eyes narrowed. "What kind of accident? You didn't run anyone over, did you?"

I narrowed my eyes back at him. Now was hardly the time to bring up my run-in with the illustrious Professor Harvey Gilmore. Harvey Gilmore is a big man in oceanographic circles. Thirty years ago he wrote a book called *Changes in the Deep* which is still a must read for all oceanography undergrads. In the thirty years since its publication, Harvey Gilmore has progressed from prominent oceanographer to drunken womanizer. This, unfortunately, did nothing to sully his reputation.

He was the man who held the purse strings on the next round of grant money for my research in California. I met with him, dressed much as I was now only drier, at a luncheon where Dr. Gilmore told me how much he admired my work. He put a hand to my knee and said that there were so few women in our field. And fewer pretty ones, he said. Then he invited me to his beach cottage in Malibu, his hand all the while snaking up my thigh. We could discuss the grant, he said. And enjoy a bit of relaxation and recreation. He winked at the word recreation and said he bet I looked fabulous in a bikini. It was at that point that I got up and took my leave. Dr.

Gilmore followed me to my car and said I should think about it. I answered him by running over his toes. The toes were broken, as was any hope of getting grant money.

"Are you going to introduce me to the senator or not?" I asked Ned. I was not willing to get into yet another tiff about the proper response to sexual harassment.

"Not. Look at you."

I had looked at me and the sad but unavoidable truth was that Ned was right. Unless I could convince the senator that my enthusiasm to understand the ocean's populations included early morning swims with the fishes, I was as sunk as the *Mona Lisa*. Yet the very fact that Ned had suggested I wasn't in any condition made it conditionally impossible for me not to at least give it a try.

I marched up to the table where the senator sat and, holding out my hand, I introduced myself. "I'm so looking forward to working with the commission," I said. The senator looked up from her coffee. She couldn't have been more startled if I'd been dressed in scuba gear.

"Dr. Silva, is it?" she asked, sounding as though she were questioning my sanity as well as my name.

I've learned over the years that the cliché 'the best offense is a good defense' has a ring of truth to it. "That's right," I answered, taking Ned's chair and helping myself to coffee. "You've had a chance to look at the grant proposal?"

The senator glanced uneasily at Ned, who stood behind me, ready to escort me out on the smallest pretense. "Dr. Anderson might have mentioned it."

"Might have?" I said, looking over my shoulder at Ned.

"The senator has a lot of important things on her plate. A dogfish study is just one of them."

"Dogfish?" asked the senator.

To which I felt my only recourse was to educate the woman from Massachusetts as to exactly what it was I was proposing. I outlined the study, the main purpose of which was to take a population count of shark so that the commissions setting fishing regulations could make informed decisions about those regulations. It was clear by the time I got halfway through my mini-lecture that the senator would not have been able to tell a shark from a spotted owl. Moreover, that she did not care to make the distinction.

"I'll see what we can do." The senator put her napkin carefully on her plate.

"It's very important," I emphasized again. "The life of the fishing community depends on it."

"Well then," the senator checked her watch. "I've got to be moving along. Beverly was quite impressed with this place. I'm sorry she couldn't be here."

"Beverly?" I asked

"My daughter," said the senator. "She wants to have the wedding here. She likes to get my opinion on things, wanted me to see it. So I agreed. A field trip to the Cape is a pleasant proposition after all. Pretty here in spring." The senator looked me in the eye.

"And the locals are quite colorful."

"Beverly Santos is the senator's daughter?" I asked Ned, once the senator had driven off. Beverly Santos was Ned's assistant. She was twenty-two and had the body of a well-endowed Greek goddess.

"Santos is her father's name," said Ned.

"I don't give a damn," I said. "Let me get this straight, the only reason the senator came to the Cape was to case out the Provincetown Inn for a wedding reception?"

"Not the only reason. I gave the grant proposal to her intern. I arranged for you to meet with her. She's a busy woman, but the proposal will get read. Not that it needs to, now that you've given the full report yourself."

"I thought we were here to discuss the grant proposal. It's difficult to discuss a grant proposal you haven't read."

Before Ned could answer me, his cell phone rang. He walked off to answer it, though I couldn't help overhearing snatches of the conversation. "Hi, sweetheart. Yes....She loved it...It will be fine...About two hundred guests?"

Either Ned had become Beverly Santos's wedding planner or... It hit me like a thunderbolt. "So, who's the lucky groom?" I asked Ned once he'd gotten off the phone.

"Groom?" Ned eyed my car keys. No doubt wondering if I could control my impulses.

I wasn't sure that I could. "Were you going to tell me?"

"Of course I was. Not that you and I.... We're divorced, Nikki. It was only a matter of time until one of us..."

"Cheated on their fiancé?" I offered. I told Ned, in no uncertain terms, exactly what I thought of him. And I also may have threatened to call the lovely and buxom Beverly to inform her as to exactly what she was getting herself into.

"You wouldn't," said Ned.

To which I got into my truck and started the engine. And nearly ran Ned over, but only because he stood in front of the truck with his arms out.

I pulled the parking brake and got back out. "Despite whatever delusions of grandeur you may have, you are not a superhero," I told him. "And if I wasn't so averse to spending the rest of my life dribbling a basketball in a prison yard, you'd be dead about now."

"You haven't changed, babe."

I slapped him. Hard. "I guess you'll say I deserved that." I got back in the truck. "I'll make it up to you," he said, grabbing the door before I could slam it shut.

"How?"

"I'll make sure the senator reads your proposal."

"When?"

"Soon."

I took off the parking brake and put the truck in drive.

"I'll figure out something."

"You better figure something out," I said, giving him the 'don't mess with me' stare I'd learned by virtue of having three younger brothers. Then I shut the door and drove off, wishing the lot hadn't been paved so that I

could have left Ned standing in the dust.

Chapter Four

Marco

Angie brought me over to the Lincoln that Phil had parked out back of Roma's. The car could have featured in a gangster movie, big and black, with tinted windows. Unlike in the movies, Angie opened the passenger door in front and told me to get in. Since he was the one with a gun I wasn't about to question his methods. We wound through downtown and got on the Jersey turnpike. Angie turned the TomTom on and a woman with an English accent started saying things like "stay in the center lane," which added to the sense I had that if I pinched myself I'd wake up on the cot in the storage room of Roma's.

"What were you thinking?" Angie said, as we headed away from Newark towards Manhattan.

"Where are we going?"

"Jesus and Mary, what were you thinking getting mixed up with a girl like Lark Lazario?"

"She told me she was pregnant. I wanted to do the right thing by her."

"Jesus and Joe, what are you, a choir boy? Girls like that don't get in the family way by accident and if they do, they take care of it."

"Fat Phil is a good Catholic."

Angie gave me a look like I just jumped from the crazy train. "You were thinking with your fire hose instead of your noodle. You're no kid. I would a thought you knew better."

Damned if he wasn't right. Because if I'd have been thinking straight I never would have been fool enough to get tangled up with Lark.

I had banged around for a long time after I left my home in Trenton and decided to make it big in the Big Apple. A couple of years of community college and I was gonna rule the world. I got work as a dishwasher in this little joint down in Tribeca and since the so-called chef was hung over most mornings, he let me do the prep work. Which was how I figured out I liked to cook. I was damn good at it, too. So I saved my pennies, went to cooking school, and got a real job as a sous chef in a nice place Mid-town. I spent the next ten years cooking at different places and drinking at the bars of those places and meeting a lot of women.

Then I met Lark. It wasn't strangers across a crowded room, understand. I didn't get hit by a lightning bolt or anything like that. She was just another hot girl sitting in this bar, Rudy's, where I was working at the time. A week after we hooked up, I found out her daddy was one of the biggest mob bosses outside the city. Three weeks later, she called me out of the blue crying her eyes out. Said she needed to talk to me. So I met her down in a local diner and there sitting next to her was

Phil, with this big medallion hanging from what ought to be a neck and a big bulge in his jacket that wasn't a wallet.

Lark was sniffling into a napkin and Phil said that I got her in trouble. Swear to God, took me a minute to catch his meaning.

"You do right by her," Phil said. Then he said that he'd set me up nice, in this little place. And I could almost see it. Not that I wanted to marry Lark, but maybe it was time to settle down, you know? And besides, when a guy like Fat Phil demands you do right by his daughter, it doesn't seem you have much of a choice. 'Course, I found out she wasn't pregnant. She told me when I caught her in bed with three burly guys. You'd have thought I would have figured it out sooner.

"You're right. I'm a moron," I said.

"Fucking moron," said Angie, nodding in agreement.

"I don't even know what Phil was talking about. All I know from Vlad is that he drinks Stoli on the rocks."

"I thought you was smart. You went to college, right?"

"Community college," I said, as though maybe that would excuse my getting mixed up with Phil and company.

Angie sighed and began talking slow, like I was a kindergarten kid and he was teaching me the alphabet. "Vlad's got an escort service. Imports girls from Eastern Europe."

"And so?"

"Think, Marco."

And just like that, the coin dropped. All

those late nights when I'd get home before Lark though it was 2:00 in the morning. She'd tell me she was out with her girlfriends. I was putting a lot of time into Roma's, not paying much attention. "Lark?" I said. "Lark's running a game with the Russians? Her father's rivals?"

"She don't get on with the old man as well as you think. Phil catches wind of what's going on and..."

"Lark set me up for the fall. She threw me under the fucking bus."

"She was working you from the start. Months ago, Phil first started sniffing the air."

"Holy shit, I am a moron."

Angie shook his head. "Nah, you got hosed. Could a happened to anybody."

"Look, you don't want to off an innocent man, do you? I know I'm an idiot but Jesus and Mary, is that a good enough reason to put me on ice?"

"I don't want to," Angie said.

"So don't. Don't do it. All you got to do is drop me off in Times Square and let bygones be bygones."

"What are you, loco? This is Fat Phil we're talking about."

We were coming up on the tollbooth for the George Washington Bridge. What they say about New York never sleeping is true. It was nearly midnight, but the toll plaza was jammed up with traffic, most of it big trucks hauling the next day's wares to the city. Angie rooted through his pocket and came up with a quarter and two lint-covered pennies.

"You got any ones?" he asked.

"Excuse me?"

"I need cash to pay the toll. This car don't have E-Zpass and they don't take credit. So, you got any money?"

"Let me get this straight. You want me to pay the toll so that you can dump me in the East River?"

"You don't have to put it that way."

"What way you want me to put it?"

"You got money or no?"

"No."

"Hand me your wallet."

"Let me get this straight. You want me to hand you my wallet so that...?"

Angie patted the piece under his jacket. "Don't go making this difficult."

What could I do? I handed him my wallet. He started riffling through it. "Jesus and Mary, I thought you said you was going to the bank."

"You thought wrong," I lied. I grew up in Trenton and had lived in New York most of my life. Wallets were what muggers and hit men snatched from you. Last place you want to keep your money.

Angie pulled out a handful of ones and started counting as a WalMart double trailer pulled up to the right of us. "You got five ones here. Toll is eight bucks. Where am I supposed to come up with three bucks?" We were surrounded by a wall of trucks. Angie was checking his pockets for more loose change. I opened the door and jumped out.

"Hey," I heard Angie yell as I skirted the WalMart truck's cab. Car horns started to beep. I ran over onto the pedestrian walk on the bridge. I ran until my sides hurt and I kept on running away from Jersey as though my life depended on it, because it did.

Chapter Five

Nikki

It never occurred to me that Rusty's marina would make the evening news, but there it was— the lead story on Channel Five at 5:00. And there was Rusty, still dazed from our morning plunge, being interviewed.

"I don't know what happened. One minute I was on the boat and the next, kaboom!" he told the pretty blonde reporter.

Not that anyone in P-town needed a television. While I had gone home, washed the rest of the sand from my hair, and changed into fresh clothes, my father had been down at Ella's Place getting an earful of gossip from the other retired fishermen.

"What in Jesus's name did you do, girl?" Pop asked the minute I walked through the door after having gone to the Stop & Shop to pick up something for dinner. I handed him one of the two grocery sacks I was carrying. "Blow up a marina, that's a new one"

"Burgers or ravioli?" If there was one thing that could take Pop's mind off kaboom! it was food.

"Burgers."

Grateful that my ploy had worked, I grabbed a pan from the cupboard. Which caused a chain reaction that sent three pot lids and a cookie sheet crashing to the floor.

"You got to organize them." Pop picked up a pot lid and shoved it back into the cupboard. "How many times I got to tell you?"

I put the pan on the stove and turned on the gas, in an unfortunate re-enactment of the cause of the boat demise. Pop turned the burner off and for a moment I was sure he was going to lecture me on gas and bees, but he said, "Hamburger goes for what? Three bucks a pound and you want to go and fry it up. You ought to have to announce that at confession."

I put the pan back into the cupboard. "You'll need it for the fries," Pop said.

"I bought potato salad." I held up the container.

"At the deli? How much that set you back?"

"Fine." I stuffed the salad container back into the grocery sack. "I'll take it back and get a refund."

Pop took the container back out. "What else you got?"

"Those Kalamata olives you like. I can take them back too if they're too expensive."

"So," Pop took out two plates and set them on the kitchen table, "how for the love of God you get Rusty to blow up his inventory?"

Chapter Six

Marco

I felt like fate was giving me the finger. There I was, running across the George Washington Bridge, trying to listen behind me for the clop of Angelo's big feet or gunshots or whatever it was that would be the last sound I ever heard. But just as you start to curse the finger of fate, there's a sign. In my case, a sign that said 'NYC Port Authority: George Washington Bridge Bus Terminal.'

Like Frank once crooned, if I could make it there I could make it anywhere. I picked up my pace and by the time I got off the bridge and to the terminal entrance, I was wheezing as hard as a six-pack-a-day smoker. I considered my options as I caught my breath. There were signs for the subway into midtown, but despite the fact that New York was a big town, Fat Phil's organization had long arms and I didn't want to risk getting found. I saw another sign for the bus terminal pointing up the stairs. I ran up to the terminal for the Red and Tan line buses. It was the middle of the night, so there weren't a lot of departures and arrivals. In fact, the only departure listed left in an hour. And it was going to Jersey City. Even if I could hide out for an hour, back to New Jersey was about the last place I wanted to go.

There was fate, flipping me the bird again. I was about to run downstairs and take my chances with the A train, when I heard talking out on the platform. And standing there, like a refrigerator full of cold beer for a thirsty man, was a charter bus. The driver was loading suitcases onto the bus and people were queued up and boarding. I got on line and pretty soon I found a seat. I had no idea as to where it was that I was going, but I knew that if it was far enough away for a suitcase, it must be out of the Tri-State area.

I was about to sit down when someone tapped me on the shoulder. State I was in, this about sent me through the roof. I turned and there stood a black man with a big bald head came up to about my chin. He was smiling, but I could tell that he was not real happy with me. "What are you doing on this bus?"

"Bus?" I said, like I wasn't familiar with the word.

The man crossed his arms and the hairy eyeball got hairier. People were jostling to get around him, so he stepped into the seat in front of me, staring me down the whole time. "You are not one of us," he said. "I'd know. I arranged this trip and I would remember you."

"Calvin." A manicured hand came up from the seat by the window next to the man and touched him on the elbow. "Settle down, sweetheart. You're getting all tense again." The hand's owner popped up out of the seat and turned, revealing a tall skinny guy so pale he could have been an extra in that movie about vampires. He was wearing a pink silk shirt, a purple silk scarf, and eyeliner. "Don't mind him," the man said to me. He took his hand from Calvin's elbow and held it out to shake mine. "I'm Evan," he said. "And you are?" With his other hand he started giving Calvin a neck massage.

"On my bus," said Calvin. Evan gave Calvin a little slap and told him to behave. "So," said Evan. "Why are you on our bus?"

"I'm new," I said.

Calvin, who seemed to be going into a hypnotic trance with Evan's neck massage, snapped out of it at the sound of my voice. "New my ass. He's not on my list. I know everybody on that list and he's not on it. He's a stowaway." The bus lurched forward and began moving away from the platform.

"I'm sure he has his reasons." Evan looked me over. "Well, come on, out with it, what are your reasons?"

I wasn't about to say I was running from a hit man who was trying to kill me. That would have made for a lot of explaining. "I'm a friend." Now that just made me sound like I was nuts. But, hell, I had a hit man chasing me. Maybe I was nuts.

Calvin raised his eyebrows and I figured he was about to yell to the driver to stop the bus and they'd dump me out alongside Interstate 95. "I can pay," I took the money clip I had—impressive looking with two hundred dollars in twenties—from the inside pocket of my jacket. "How much for a ticket?"

"He can pay," said Evan to Calvin. "You see, he's an honest boy." "He didn't reserve a seat," said Calvin.

"Calvin, honey," Evan began with the massage again. "How many seats are on this bus?"

"Fifty-seven."

"And how many seats did the Greater Teaneck Gay Men's Choir reserve?"

"Forty-two," said Calvin. I got to say, he looked disappointed.

"So there are mucho plenty of seats available, am I right or wrong?"

"You're right."

"And this sweet, sweet man wants to pay for one of those seats. We could use the money for a new pitch pipe."

"Fine." Calvin, held out his hand like a bellhop waiting for a tip. "One sixty for the trip."

"One hundred sixty bucks?" The confidence that started leaking when Evan said 'gay men's choir' might as well have gotten left alongside the highway like a blown out truck tire.

"It's round trip. Five and a half hours each way. And we have to pay the driver extra because it's overnight." Calvin began with the hairy eyeball again.

I counted out eight of my ten twenties and slid them into Calvin's outstretched palm.

"Have a nice ride," Calvin said. I was pretty sure he didn't mean it.

No one had taken the seat next to me. This was a good thing, because I was in no mood for polite conversation. I'd managed to get out of New York but now I was on a bus full of gay men in the middle of the night. A bus that was speeding at sixty miles an hour to an unknown destination five and a half hours away. I had no driver's license and no bank cards. If the bus was in a head-on collision, my body would be identified as John Doe, the guy who had forty bucks in his pocket.

"New Haven, home of the Whiffenpoofs," Evan said, taking the aisle seat beside mine. He pointed out the window to a sign for the exit to New Haven, Connecticut. "A cappella singing group at Yale. They are fabulous. Calvin was a Whiffenpoof." Evan put his hand on my arm. "You have to excuse Calvin. He gets all tight in the drawers every time he organizes a trip. Don't do it anymore, I tell him. It's not worth the heart attack. But Calvin loves to be in charge. Though you wouldn't know it now. He's out like the little light that could."

"It's okay," I said, staring at Evan's fingers.

Evan pulled his hand from my arm and set to ironing out the imaginary creases in his chinos. "So, if you're not part of the Greater Teaneck Gay Men's Choir, who are you?"

Good question. Who was I? Maybe all of this was God's way of saying I ought to start over. A clean slate. Sunrise on a new day without a mob boss or a hit man in sight.

"Sorry," said Evan. "It's none of my beeswax."

"I can't sing," I said.

"You can sing in my choir loft any day."

Evan beamed at me. "Sorry," he said again. "It's a bad habit. Flirt reflex. It kicks in when tall, dark, and handsome strangers get on my bus. But I can see that I'm making you uncomfortable."

"No, it's fine. A little flirting, what's the big deal?" I said, because he was making me damned uncomfortable.

"But you're not gay."

"How would you know that?"

Evan shrugged. "A hunch. Really, you just don't seem gay, that's all."

"What if I was? Gay?"

Evan raised his eyebrows. "Then I'd say you're going to the right place."

"The right place?"

I was going to ask Evan what he meant when he said, "I take it you've never been to Provincetown?"

Chapter Seven

Nikki

"So, how many boats did Rusty blow up for you?" asked my brother Billy the next day. I had just come from Ella's Place, where I'd been ribbed about Rusty over a poached egg and an English muffin, and was meeting Billy at the Red Tomato. Let me rephrase: I was meeting Billy at what would someday become the Red Tomato, which Billy hoped would someday be the finest eating establishment in the east end of P-town.

"Great ambiance," I said, getting out of my car in the weed-strewn parking lot. I might have said it a bit sarcastically, but I wanted Billy to know I was done with being poked in the behind about Rusty.

"I know what you're thinking," Billy said. He waded through the dune grass to the Tomato's front door. The building, what was left of it, was, as Billy had often reminded me, a landmark. It had been the site of Land's End, which had been one of the finest eating establishments in town. When Pop was a kid. By the time I hit adolescence, the place had become an aged silhouette of its previous self. By the time Billy hit adolescence, it had become a deserted old building on the dunes.

Which pretty well summed up where things stood. The dunes all around had begun reclaiming the place. A pile of sand lay banked against a windswept wall, the roof had caved just above and dipped into the sand. The front walk was a flattened path through dune grass and the scarred door stood slightly off its hinges.

"You have no idea what I'm thinking," I said, following him. Although I'm sure Billy knew that along with our other brothers, Harry and Pete, I thought this was his most foolish enterprise to date. And Billy had a long list of foolish enterprises. He was twenty-five and had already worked his way through three businesses. The last of which, a combination dog grooming parlor and nail salon, had set my brothers and me back several thousand dollars in investment money. Pop had refused to give Billy any funding because by the time the salon idea came along, Billy had come out of the closet.

"At least it won't cost you anything this time." Billy knew more about what I was thinking than I cared to admit.

What Billy had said was true enough. Billy's boyfriend, Jeremy Fine, would be funding the brunt of the restoration. My other brothers and I had no problem with Billy being gay. His choice of partner, however, was another story all together. The only positive thing I could find to say about Jeremy Fine was that he had money and didn't mind sharing it with my baby brother. Harry and Pete would say that Jeremy might have money, but he spent it like water, and someday the well was going to go dry, leaving Billy penniless once again. Buying and restoring Land's End was a case in point.

Billy opened the door, which fell off the bottom hinge, to a dark vestibule. Beyond that was a bar with a cracked mirror running the length of the wall behind it and festooned in Christmas lights that must have been several decades old. A single table sat in the middle of the scuffed and sand- covered dining room floor and at the table sat Jeremy, his balding blond head bent over a blueprint, with a woman I didn't recognize.

Jeremy jumped up when we walked in, kissed Billy on the cheek, and took me by both shoulders. "Nicola! Just the woman I wanted to see." He brought us over to the table and introduced the woman sitting as Sarah Simon, Boston's premier architect and "the woman who will restore this place to glory. Nay, who will make it the most glorious spot in all of Massachusetts."

"I wouldn't go that far." Ms. Simon was obviously unaccustomed to Jeremy's hyperbole.

Ignoring the comment, Jeremy took me by the arm and led me to a boarded-up window. "Sweeping view of the dunes through wall-to-wall glass," he said. "Outside seating on a charming patio."

"You'll get sand in the food," I said. To which I heard Ms. Simon chuckle.

Jeremy waltzed over to the bar where Billy stood and rapped on the bar top. "Solid oak. Worth a small fortune. Ditto the floors," he said, tapping a toe against a loose board.

He pointed to a set of scarred double doors along one side, "The kitchen is a horror, but it will be state of the art once we're through. By Memorial Day this place will be memorable."

I nearly choked on the sand. Memorial Day was six weeks away. Ms. Simon must have shared the sentiment. "I'm not sure," she began.

"I know." Jeremy threw his hands to the beamed and cobwebbed ceiling. "I know. So little time, so much to do. But we will make it happen."

Ms. Simon looked to the notes she had been taking and shook her head. I had the thought that memorable wasn't necessarily good.

"And if it doesn't work out, Nik can blow the place up," said Billy, leaning against the bar rail.

"For God sake," I said, "I didn't blow up Rusty's boat."

"You do make Rusty nervous, though," said Billy, sounding exactly like Pete and Harry. My brother Harry also had suggested that I turned Rusty into a trembling bowl of Jell-O.

"Yeah, he's a wreck around you," Pete had seconded.

"He's married. He has four kids," I said.

"Has nothing to do with it," said Harry, who called over his wife, Ella. Since she owned Ella's Place and gave us all free breakfast, Harry claimed she could be the deciding factor. Ella came over, poured us more coffee, and agreed that Rusty was a wreck around me. "The Chappaquiddick," the three of them had said in unison.

"Did I ever tell you about the Chappaquiddick?" Billy asked Jeremy.

"You were five years old," I said.

"I've seen the tape. Harry shows it every January twenty-first, on the anniversary," said Billy.

Harry did not show the tape every January. But the truth of the matter was that Harry did have in his possession a tape of Rusty Cook who, nearly twenty years ago in a panic strewn moment during driver's ed, had hit the gas instead of the brake and had nearly sent the student driver's car diving off Macmillan Pier. Fortunately, the driver's ed instructor, Mr. Dumont, had a brake on his side of the vehicle, which saved our rear tires from plunging past the pilings. I say 'our' because, unfortunately, I had been in the backseat at the time. There was, and still is, a surveillance camera at the pier which documented the incident. Hence the tape, that my brother Harry somehow bribed Joey Dyer into selling.

I surmised, as I had for nearly twenty years, that I couldn't help it if Rusty Cook was a klutz. My brothers surmised that I made Rusty jumpy and always had. I had finally begun to live down the Chappaquiddick when along came the *Mona Lisa*, which I would no doubt hear about for the next twenty years. At least there is no tape of the incident. As far as I know.

"Poor *Mona*, gone to the great boatyard in the sky," said Billy as Jeremy said "Not to worry, my dear madame, I have come to your rescue."

"Terrific," I said.

"It just so happens I have a boat. You need a boat and I have a boat. It's kismet."

"You have a boat? What kind of a boat?"

"A fabulous boat. Pleasure cruiser," sang Jeremy.

"And how is it that I don't know you have a boat?"

"Because I bought it this morning! It is bobbing to the harbor as we speak."

"You bought a boat?"

"Forty-footer," said Billy, knowing I'd be impressed.

"You bought a forty-foot boat?"

"Yes, darling. You need a boat. I have a boat."

"What's wrong with this picture?" I said.

"Nothing's wrong," said Billy. "Jeez, Nik."

"All I want," said Jeremy, "is your unending happiness."

"And what else?'

"And," said Jeremy, "the unending happiness of my darling boy."

"And?"

"We've been invited to Ella's Easter tadoodle," said Billy. Ella was having a family get together for Easter tomorrow.

"But you aren't coming," I said.

"Au contraire," said Jeremy.

"Why not?" said Billy. "I love Jeremy and I want my family to love him, too. All we ask is that you stand behind us. Ella agrees."

It was just like Ella. Make enough macaroni salad and feed all the warring factions. Not that I didn't agree that fences needed mending. But Pop was likely to blow a gasket and God only knew what Aunt Viddie would do.

The thing is, Pop hadn't spoken to Billy since he came out last year. Which was unacceptable and also ridiculous when you consider that Pop had lived in Provincetown his whole life and gays were as prevalent in my home town as sea gulls. But Pop was set in his ways. He'd come around to having a gay son sooner or later, or so we all hoped. And he probably would have by now if not for Jeremy. Pop would accept Billy, but he might never abide Jeremy.

Pop's sister, our Aunt Viddie, believed that homosexuality was an affliction and that Billy had caught the disease the summer he worked at Spiritos Pizza as a dishwasher. It must have been the dishwater, she surmised. She would shake her head and say "poor boy" whenever Billy's name was mentioned. Since common sense was not Viddie's strong suit, trying to disavow our aunt of her notion was a little like trying to tell the rain not to fall.

Ella closed Ella's Place after lunch. I caught her just as she was about to lock the door.

"Why?" I said. To which she unlocked the door and put on a pot of coffee.

"Somebody had to do it."

"But both of them? Billy alone, I get.

But Jeremy?"

"It's time. I'm tired of tiptoeing around your father."

"Easy for you to say. Your folks moved to Boca Raton."

"Come on, Nik. You and I both know it's stupid, this fight. Pop has to get over it. He can't just pretend Billy doesn't exist. Harry agrees and so do you."

"Hello, have you met our father? He hasn't set foot in the Stop & Shop since they bought out the A&P. He still takes it personally that they raised docking fees twenty years ago. He hasn't spoken to Fred Shaw since, and Fred isn't even the harbor master anymore."

"This isn't the A&P or fishing, Nik. This is Billy we're talking about."

Of course, Ella was right. Though that was not about to make tomorrow's shindig any easier.

Chapter Eight

Marco

As we drove through Connecticut and into Rhode Island, Evan chatted on about how the Greater Teaneck Gay Men's Choir did a Sunrise in Provincetown trip each spring. They rode a charter bus all night long through New England to the far end of Cape Cod, where they joined up with the Provincetown Gay Men's Choir to sing at sunrise Easter services at the Universalist Unitarian Meeting House. Then, Evan said, they would spend the remainder of their time in P-town 'vacationing their asses off,' until it was time to board the bus back to New Jersey on Monday afternoon.

Evan fell asleep as we drove through southeastern Massachusetts.

And I began thinking that maybe fate wasn't such a nasty bitch after all. Fat Phil might believe that I was a liar and a cheat, but the idea that I was gay would never cross his mind. Hell, the idea that I was gay had never crossed *my* mind. Provincetown, according to Evan, was a Mecca for gay men. It would be easy to fade into the gay community. I could get a job, an apartment...

Then I glanced over at Evan and had second thoughts. He was a sweet guy and I owed him a debt of gratitude for saving my hide. But I couldn't imagine getting romantic with him. I'd have to figure out some reason for not having a love life.

By the time the bus crossed the bridge at Buzzard's Bay and headed up the Cape, I had concocted a story. I was moving to Provincetown with my boyfriend, Murray. Only Murray couldn't join me right away on account of the fact that he was Canadian. Since Fat Phil might be inclined to look for a chef, I figured I needed a new job. Provincetown was surrounded by ocean. Ocean had fish in it. So Murray and I were fishermen, looking to start a new life in a place where we could fish and be gay and be left in peace. By the time the bus rolled into P-town, I had myself convinced that it would all work out.

After the bus dropped us off and Evan got the boys to sing "So Long, Farewell," as we went our separate ways, I had to stop myself from flagging down another bus and begging the driver to take me back to Newark.

I walked the length of Commercial Street. Most of the shops were still closed and the only noise came from the pier where the boats were going in and out and off into distance. Church bells started to ring, and I thought about my Nona and how all those years she'd drag me off to Mass every week and how on Easter she'd always hide a couple of those plastic Easter eggs with pennies in them. I was a sucker for those eggs. I don't think she would've liked it to see me walking down the street homeless, so I made her a promise that I'd find a job. And that, after I got done with being gay, I'd settle down with a nice girl.

I remembered Evan's words about my not seeming gay, so every time I saw two men together I watched real careful so I could imitate. I've always been good with imitation; I was in the drama club back in high school. By the time I got back to the pier, I had the walk down pretty good. Subtle, not too obvious, just enough of a swagger to sell it.

I sat on a bench and watched the boats go by and I was feeling better about my prospects. The smell of fish came up from the pier and I got to thinking how it was the smell of a whole new life and that I could get used to this. Tomorrow, I'd go off in search of a job, but for now I'd just sit on the bench and enjoy the warm weather. I let my thoughts wander around for a while, watching the seagulls wheel around and thinking maybe I should practice being gay some more when they walked past, two men holding hands and the most gorgeous red-haired woman I ever laid eyes on.

Like I said, when I met Lark I wasn't struck by a thunderbolt. I'm not real proud of myself, but I was on that night just trying to score. Had you asked before that minute when the redhead walked past, I would have said that the whole thunderbolt thing was a myth; that no man on earth, to my knowledge and experience, had ever been struck that way. I would have kept on believing that, too, but the redhead looked at me with these big brown eyes. Her hair was wavy and the sun played on it like you'd want to write a poem about it. Then she smiled this smile like she'd known me all my life and Jesus, God, I was hit by it. The thunderbolt. No kidding.

One of the men said something that made her laugh, and what a laugh, like pearls falling to the floor. I should have said something, but it was like my tongue was caught in my throat and I was paralyzed.

I watched them walk away and she had the most graceful walk I ever saw. She was small, maybe five three or four and the one guy who wasn't much taller must have been related to her because he had the same coppery hair. Then the other man put his arm around the copper-haired man and I remembered that I was supposed to be gay.

And I thought to myself that this gay thing was going to be harder to pull off than I'd thought.

Chapter Nine

Nikki

"Oooh, muffin alert. Over on the bench," Jeremy said. "Good thing I'm taken."

Billy and I turned in unison to look back. The man stared back at us with a pair of emerald eyes that stopped my breath for a minute. He had curly dark hair and a face that looked as though Michelangelo had carved it. "Not bad," said Billy, shoving in to me.

I turned again, just briefly, to see him walk away. The walk told it all. "Gay," I surmised.

"Maybe," said Billy, also watching.

"Definitely," said Jeremy, grabbing Billy by the shoulders. "Not that it matters."

"No," I said. "Not that it matters."

Thoughts of the mystery man all but disappeared when Jeremy, with the sort of enthusiasm that only Jeremy could muster, began pointing. "There she is," he said.

I followed the pointed finger and laid my eyes on Jeremy's latest acquisition. "The *P-town Queen?*"

"Is she not the most beautiful thing you've ever seen?"

"She's purple," I said, shooting Billy a look meant to send him flying off the pier.

Billy shrugged it off and, as though to catch himself in slow motion, took hold of my arm and sighed an exasperated sigh. "So what? She's big. She's new. She's clean."

"Brand new," said Jeremy. "A mere baby boat."

We climbed aboard and she did look good. Big and new and clean, as Billy had pointed out. But the *P-town Queen*? The purple *P-town Queen*? Barney the Dinosaur was supposed to be purple. Fishing vessels were not. Pop would have an aneurysm. Pete and Harry would tell me I ought to blow her up. She'd be the laughing stock of every fishing boat out on the Banks.

We followed Jeremy below deck where another surprise awaited.

The entire cabin was done in red leather, which seemed as pervasive as had the mold on the *Mona Lisa*. And on the ceiling, hanging from a chain were a pair of... "Handcuffs?" I nearly spit this out. "Please tell me those aren't handcuffs."

"It *is* a pleasure cruiser," Jeremy raised his eyebrows at pleasure in a way that made me want to squirm. "You're blushing! Slap my behind and call me the New Year's baby, I never thought I'd see Nicola Silva blush."

It was good to see that Billy was blushing, too, and that he was at least as uncomfortable as I was. But then Jeremy put his arm around Billy's shoulder and the two of them stood there as moonfaced as any couple on a honeymoon.

"Thanks for letting me borrow her," I said.

"No problemo, my fair lady," Jeremy said. "Now let's go see the relations, shall we?"

"It will be fine," said Billy, as we parked on the curb in front of the house that Ella and Harry shared with their twin sixteen-year-old sons, Ford and Lincoln, known to the family as the Cars, and my brother Pete who, since his divorce two years ago, lived in the apartment over the garage.

"You trying to convince me or yourself?" I asked. To which Billy took Jeremy's arm and said that they were going to have to face Pop sooner or later.

"But Pop and Aunt Viddie? Isn't that a little ... I don't know... suicidal?"

"Oh bite me," said Jeremy. "I'm looking forward to meeting your Auntie. She sounds amusing."

"She's amusing all right," I muttered as we came in through the front door without bothering to ring.

Ford and Linc were in the living room playing Doom. Linc stopped shooting at his brother long enough to tell us that his mother was in the kitchen with Viddie and that his father and Uncle Pete had gone to the market.

"Like two hours ago," added Ford, eyeing Billy and Jeremy.

We left the Cars to Armageddon and made our way to the kitchen where Ella had her head in the refrigerator and Viddie sat at the kitchen table nursing a glass of lemonade.

Which, knowing Viddie, had no doubt been quietly reinforced with gin.

Viddie looked up from her drink. "Well, look who the cat dragged in," she said, enveloping Billy and me in for a landing against her voluptuous breasts while Ella dropped a five hundred pound tub of ambrosia onto the table.

Jeremy stuck out his hand and Billy made the introduction. "I'm always glad to meet Billy's friends," said Viddie, taking the hand as though she might kiss it.

"Jeremy is Billy's special friend," said Ella. To which I shot her a look. Luckily, the comment floated somewhere near the ceiling far over Viddie's head.

"It's good to have friends, isn't it? I myself have a lot of friends. Why, the Rosary Society alone...We missed you at Mass this morning, Nikki. The lilies on the altar looked beautiful if I do say so myself. Ella said you went last night, to the vigil. Weren't they beautiful, Ella?"

"Thank you," I mouthed silently to Ella, who rolled her eyes.

"They were lovely," said Ella. "You ladies always do such a nice job."

"You should join the Society," said Aunt Viddie. "Both of you."

"Where are those paper plates?" said Ella. I helped her look though they were stacked on the counter.

"Are you a Catholic, Jeremy?" asked Viddie.

"No ma'am. Sadly, I am not."

"You're not a local boy, I'd know you if

you were."

"No, ma'am. I'm from Maryland."

"Maryland," said Viddie. "Well, isn't that wonderful." Then, not able to find anything relevant to say about Maryland, she took another sip of her drink.

Jeremy nodded. If it weren't for the pink socks you could almost have mistaken him for a straight man. Viddie, either by design or out of real ignorance, did. "And you're not married?" she said, happy to have found a way to continue the interview.

"Not yet," said Jeremy, keeping a straight face.

I found it a little harder to keep up the masquerade. I picked up the mega tub of ambrosia before Ella could get hold of it. "Porch, right?" I said.

"Why don't I show you?" said Ella.

The ambrosia caught Viddie's eye and deflected her interest in Jeremy. "You didn't put cherries in. You know that Nick," with this she looked at me, "your father," as if I didn't know which Nick she was referring to, "loves those cherries. I keep a jar right in the door of the refrigerator. They perk up a salad."

"And a drink," said Ella, under her breath.

"Maybe you should call the boys, tell them that while they're over there at the Stop & Shop they ought to pick up a jar."

"I'll do that." Ella led the way to the screen porch. "Maybe I'll march over to the store with a rifle and shoot Harry for desertion," she muttered.

Pop and Ed, who was the cook at Ella's

Place, were out on the screen porch drinking Amstel Lights.

"That looks good," said Ed.

"You forgot the cherries." Pop pulled out a marshmallow and popped it into his mouth. He stopped chewing and stared at Billy and Jeremy, who had followed us out.

"Hey, Pop," said Billy, sounding as though he were ten. "This is my friend, Jeremy."

"Think I'll see what the Cars are up to," said Pop. And he walked away, leaving Jeremy with his hand extended to no one. Ed, out of embarrassment, took the hand while Ella said, "Shit," and gave me a look.

"Oh, no," I said. I was not about to be moved. I was, as a matter of fact, about to tell her she was the one who'd made the salad, she could damn well eat it. But then I caught the look on Billy's face, as though the world had just collapsed, and I went back into the house to find Pop, who had happily intercepted Harry and taken a bag of groceries from him.

"Ketchup," said Harry, unpacking. "Extra buns. And Pete's bringing up the ice."

"Maraschinos." Viddie eyed Ella who'd come back into the kitchen. "We're all out."

"I can run back." Harry made his way back towards the door. Ella grabbed his shirt. "You leave, you die," she said, just as Pete walked in hoisting a ten pound bag of ice.

"Your father," she said to me.

"He was just here," said Harry, looking around as though Pop had vanished into thin air. He nodded towards Billy, Jeremy, and Ed, who were still out on the sun porch nodding at each other. "That have anything to do with his disappearance?" he asked.

I found Pop on the couch between the Cars, idly watching as they shot each other in virtual reality. "Linc's winning," he said as I stood in the doorway.

"How long are you going to keep this up?" I said.

"What?"

"You know damned well what," I said. It was at this point that Ford remembered that he and his brother were supposed to help set up the grill.

"You're going to ruin this for Ella," I said as the Cars left.

"Ella will get over it. She'll have another tadoodle for the blessing come June."

"And Billy will come and bring Jeremy."

"So maybe I'll stay to home."

"Maybe you'll stop being a stubborn old coot and be a good father to your son."

"You listen here, little girl. I raised that kid alone when your mother died. Don't you go telling me about being a father." My mother had died when I was twenty and Bill was ten. Pop could still make me feel the sting of that, even now.

"If Mama were here, she'd tell you to get your sorry carcass in there and make it up with her baby boy and his friend."

I knew I had him. Because Pop knew as well as I did that Mama would never have disowned Billy. She'd love Billy no matter what. She would never have held a grudge and we both knew it.

"Fine." Pop got off the couch like a man about to be sentenced. "Lead me to my doom and damnation."

Ella had set all the salads on the table and Harry was outside on the patio, grilling burgers and chicken while Jeremy and Billy and Pete sat in lawn chairs by the cooler, Jeremy regaling them with dreams of the Red Tomato.

Pop went to the cooler without a word and Jeremy asked him politely if he'd care for a glass of the white wine he'd brought. To which Pop shot him a look that would have made anyone not within earshot think Jeremy had offered up cat pee instead of chardonnay.

"Pop is more of a beer drinker," said Harry, who, busy with flipping, had missed the look.

"That's right," said Pop. "All the men in this family like beer."

"Meat's done," Harry shouted towards the porch and all of us made our way to the table. We all got settled in, Pop and Viddie on one end and Billy and Jeremy at the other, and I thought that maybe we could get through supper unscathed.

And we might have, had not Jeremy stood up and raised his glass in a toast. "It is such a pleasure to be here among family and friends," he said. He put a hand on Billy's shoulder. "I love this fella right here and I promise to take good care of him, come what may. Rain, sleet, fog, hale, I will be true." Billy shifted a little uncomfortably. Harry closed his eyes and shook his head. Pop stared at the ring his beer bottle had made on the paper table cloth.

"Any hoo," said Jeremy, completely oblivious to the uncomfortable quiet. "Bill and I have an announcement." Jeremy raised the glass like a priest during the liturgy. "I asked and he said yes. We are getting married!"

Harry had a bit of a coughing fit while Viddie said, "Who's getting married, dear?"

"Billy and Jeremy," said Ella, passing her the coleslaw.

"But they're both...oh, my," said Viddie, passing a horrified look to Pop. "Did you know about this?"

Pop threw down the paper Easter bunny napkin that he was about to tuck under his chin. "That just tears it," he muttered, and he stormed outside and marched off in the direction of our house, three blocks down.

"Maybe we should go get him," said Pete, an hour later. Jeremy had locked himself into the car and the rest of us watched from the picture window in the living room as Billy talked him into opening the passenger side door and the two of them sped off.

"Jeremy or Pop?" I asked. We had sat back down and picked at our supper, after which both Ed and the Cars muttered about some other engagement and were excused without a fight. I helped myself to another glass of wine. Ella and I had finished the first bottle and were well into killing a second.

"You never should have invited them," said Harry to Ella. "I told you it was like lighting a match into a patch of gasoline. But do you listen?"

"Shut up, Harry," said Ella. "At least I make an effort to keep the family together."

"Good job," said Harry, to which Ella called him a bastard and stomped off to the kitchen.

"Can they get married?" asked Viddie. "I didn't think they could get married."

I left my brothers to explain the finer points of Massachusetts law to Aunt Viddie and went into the kitchen. Ella was scrubbing a pot with steel wool. "You're going to scrub a hole into that thing," I told her, picking up a dishtowel.

Ella handed me the pot and went to the fridge, where she pulled out a baking dish. "I don't suppose anybody's going to want bread pudding." She put the dish down and went back to the fridge for a tub of whipped cream. "Plate?"

"No." I got two tablespoons out of the drawer and handed one to Ella.

Ella dunked her spoon deep into the pudding. "This is Harry's favorite," she said, shoveling out a huge chunk and putting it in her mouth.

"You know what would go good?" I shoveled out my own chunk. "Wine."

Ella looked towards the porch. "I'm not going to get it."

"Amaretto?" I said, checking through Ella's above-the-sink bar collection.

"Lovely."

Two glasses and half a baked dish of bread pudding later, Viddie waltzed in to say her goodbyes. "What a thing!"

Ella shoved the half-empty pan in Viddie's direction. "Want some?"

Viddie shook her head. "Two men married. Now I've heard everything. Commitment Ceremony, says Harry. I say they ought to commit themselves to the Lord, is what they ought to do." Viddie took a tissue from her purse and wiped her brow. "If you ask me, that Jeremy has led our Billy astray."

"Yes, Viddie," I said. "I'm sure that's it."

"Well, I'll pray for him," said Viddie.

"You do that, Viddie," said Ella, taking another swig of Amaretto.

I've known Ella since elementary school and Harry since I was old enough to sit up. I've known them as a couple for over twenty years and what I know best about them is this: they are both stubborn as two old men in a rowboat, but they don't stay mad. Oh, they act a good game. Ella will stomp off to Hyannis to spend the night with her sister. And once, a couple of years back, Harry spent a week sleeping on his boat, the *Two Sons*, while it was berthed on MacMillan Pier. But in the end he came home contrite and smelling of cod, and when he did, Ella poured him a cup of coffee and fried him up a couple of eggs.

So I wasn't surprised when, after Viddie clattered off with two large Tupperware bowls, that Harry came in looking dogged and Ella offered up what was left of the desecrated bread pudding and the spoon she'd been using. Pete, following in on Harry's heels, poured himself and Harry each a snifter full of Amaretto and the four of us commenced with setting the world to rights.

"I can't believe," said Ella, running her finger along the rim of the near-empty Cool Whip container, "that Viddie could have lived in P-town her whole life and could still be so profoundly stupid about gays."

"Viddie," said Harry, pointing his spoon at his wife, "is profoundly stupid about most things."

"Except Maraschino cherries," I said, "the woman knows her Maraschinos."

"And God," Pete added. "Viddie is the leading expert on God."

"What do you think of all this, Jeremy and Billy? I mean married? It's not so much that Jeremy is a man, it's just..." Ella looked thoughtful, searching for just the right word.

"A flamer?" said Harry.

"A total queen?" said Pete.

"At least he's a rich queen," I said. "He's very generous. He bought a boat and he's letting me use it."

"Why would he buy a boat?" Pete asked.

I shrugged. "The point is, it's mine for as long as I need it."

"He's giving you a boat?" Harry asked.

"Letting me use it," I said. "The boat is his."

"So, what's wrong with her?" asked Ella, ever the practical one. "Nothing."

"Uh huh." Pete took the salt and pepper

shakers from me. I realized with some small sense of horror that I had been shaking them in either hand.

"She's a great boat. Forty footer. I went to look at her today. She's brand new."

"That new boat down on the wharf? The *P-town Queen*?" Harry asked. When I didn't answer, he started to laugh and Pete asked him what was so funny.

"She's purple," said Harry. "And I don't mean purple trim, either. I mean the whole damned deck is a pretty shade of purple. And the lettering's pink."

"So what?" I said. "She's brand new and she's a forty-footer."

"She's more a flamer than Jeremy Fine," said Harry. "I bet she attracts flamers."

"She's a damned sight better than that tub Rusty was offering up," I said, feeling a little heated.

"True," said Pete. "And you haven't blown her up yet. Something to be said for that."

Chapter Ten

Marco

Sleeping on the beach might sound like some wonderful romantic notion. I had had that kind of a notion myself until I did it for real. I walked all the way out of town to what they call the dune lands, then through the dunes to where the beach is at Race Point. I stood there in the dune grass and watched the endless roll of waves and, swear to God, it felt like some sort of epiphany. I knew then and there that I had been missing something, had spent too many years holed up between musty plywood walls and spent too much time on bar stools. I was missing a whole bright world. A world, I thought, where fishermen live. Like the one I was going to be in this new life of mine.

Like I said, the place was dripping with romance. The sun set and a field of stars appeared. I lay down on my jacket gazing up at them, the surf shushing behind me, and thought how great this was. Then the wind came up and it was friggin' freezing out there on the dune. I put the jacket back on, too tired for the long hike back into town, and curled into the dune like I was some kind of small animal. I dozed like that for a while then woke up with the sand fleas biting at my face and I dozed again, on and off for the whole night. I was as grateful for the lightening gray sky as I'd been for just about anything in my thirty-six years.

I got up that morning with some new information. One, that sand makes for a scratchy and uncomfortable mattress, two, that a night out in the open leaves a man grimy and unlikely to attract company, and three, I better figure out how to change the situation before it got worse.

I walked back into town. The weather had turned cool again, and overcast. It started to drizzle as I reached a coffee shop out near the end of Bradford Street. I walked in like I owned the joint and headed straight for the john, where I washed up as best I could using the yellow soap in the dispenser and a couple of paper towels. I checked my pocket, counted out the rest of my money, nine dollars and fifty-eight cents, which, if I was lucky, would get me a cup of coffee and a hot breakfast.

It was fate making it up to me that brought me to that particular coffee shop that particular morning. Fate, because if I'd been anywhere else it never would have been Ella Silva who poured the coffee and looked me over with some concern, like I was a stray come wandering into the place.

It was fate that sent Jeremy Fine in from the rain. Of course, I didn't know who any of them were then. All I knew was that the two by two breakfast tasted damned good and that it was hot and that I was starving. I did recognize Jeremy as the guy from the dock the day before. And, as fate would have it, Jeremy recognized me, too. He gave me a kind of exaggerated wink as he walked up to the counter with a handful of flyers. I remember thinking that if anybody had the walk down, you know, the gay guy walk, it was this guy. He kind of swaggered up to the counter.

I watched the two of them, Jeremy holding out the flyers and making gestures, while Ella looked at him and the flyers like he was some kind of crazy. I was too far off to hear much, and the place was pretty busy and noisy to boot, but I did catch something like "Nick know about this?" from Ella to which Jeremy kind of shrugged. To which Ella shook her head and took the flyers Jeremy chucked at her. After Jeremy left, the grill guy came out from behind the kitchen and Ella showed him the flyers and they both laughed and shook their heads. And after that, Ella took the whole pile and stashed them out of sight behind the counter.

Seeing Jeremy reminded me of the redhead. I hate to say it, but just the thought of her put a little jolt through me again. I also got to say, it was most likely why I was so curious about those flyers. Otherwise, I would have just put them out of my mind because I had other things on my mind and there's only just so much room upstairs.

A little time passed, enough for Ella to come over and pour me a second cup of coffee, when the bell over the door let out a jingle and in walked Harry. Of course, I didn't know it was Harry back then, but he had the same wavy hair as the redhead—a little more brown than copper—so I might have guessed they were related. And, by the easy way he sat at the counter, he was surely a regular at Ella's place. This sparked my interest again and I watched as Ella showed him one of the flyers and they both had a pretty good laugh, then Harry shook his head, took one of the flyers, and stuck it in the pocket of the jacket he'd laid down on the stool next to his.

I was in no hurry to leave; the place was warm and the weather outside was damp, so I nursed the coffee. After my second cup was gone, Harry got up to leave. He went to put on his coat, and the flyer fluttered down to the floor.

This is what I was talking about. Fate. Because the flyer fell just as I was heading for the counter to pay the check. I picked it up for him and being curious, I read it. Not the whole thing, because I only got hold of it for a few seconds. But enough to see Help Wanted, Research Assistant. Apply to Dr. Silva at Fishy's T-shirt Hut.

I paid up and left my last buck fifty on the table, swearing that if I got this job, I'd come back and I'd leave a couple of extra bucks next time. I wondered what kind of research Dr. Silva was doing. I figured him for one of those goof-ball nerds you see on late night TV, you know, like Jerry Lewis. Boy, was I wrong about that one.

Chapter Eleven

Nikki

Billy called me the day after Easter and asked if I'd meet him by the Bradford Street parking lot. I found him staring into the plate glass window of Fishy's T-shirt Hut, one of your basic junky souvenir tourist traps, this one just outside the gate of the parking lot where tourists could be gotten both coming and going. Fishy's was in a converted garage, or more to the point, a deserted garage. It still had a faded Esso sign sketched over the door next to the plate glass window, which featured a display of plastic shovels and sand pails, a pink and blue stripped sand chair, and several beach balls in front of a stuffed swordfish mounted on plywood.

"Don't get mad," said Billy, eying the fish.

"That's not an auspicious beginning," I said.

"Jeremy wanted to do something for you. You know, for helping smooth the waters with Pop and Viddie."

"The waters are still pretty rough," I said.

"It's a work in progress," he said. "We get that. Anyway. Jeremy found you an office."

"An office?"

"Gordo Fish is a friend of a friend and he has a space."

I stared at my brother who was still staring at the swordfish as though it might swim off and puncture one of the beach balls. "In the T-shirt shop?"

"No, actually. Behind the shop."

"Billy, I don't need an office and I certainly don't need one in a T-shirt shop."

"Behind the shop," said Billy. "I know. I know. But you know Jeremy, he works up a head of steam and he's all excited about being your fairy Godfather."

"Emphasis on fairy."

"Thing is, he's decided he wants to help you out. So, the boat. Then he figured you needed a place to interview perspective research assistants." As he spoke, Billy led the way through the shop to a storage room in the back.

"Research assistants?"

Billy gestured to a metal desk tucked into the corner of the storage room. A tiny casement window in the cement wall offered dubious light to the corner. "You said you needed an assistant."

I shook my head. "Honey, I don't have any research."

"But you got an office." Billy pulled a metal folding chair from the wall and opened it. "That's a start, right?"

Chapter Twelve

Marco

I found Fishy's without a whole lot of trouble and asked the girl at the cash register about the job. I had turned from wondering about Dr. Silva to wondering what kind of research you did at a T-shirt hut.

"Hey, Fish," shouted the girl to a blond guy squatting over a box of snorkels, "you hiring an assistant?"

"Research assistant," I said, when Fish stopped diving into the box so he could look me over.

"You want Nick Silva." Fish pointed to an "Employees Only" sign taped onto a metal door.

I went through the door and there, in the corner of the room, was a metal desk and sitting on the desk was the redhead from the pier. I couldn't have been more surprised if it had been Fat Phil sitting there. My stomach did a loop-di-loop, like I was in the sixth grade and just found out the popular girl had the locker next to mine. I told myself to quit being a dumb ass. I had exactly two cents rubbing together in the pocket of my only pair of pants.

She was talking to the guy from the

pier. The younger one that looked like her. She caught me in her gorgeous brown eyes, blinked a few times, and asked if she could help me. "Yeah, yes," I said. "I'm here about the research. The assistant. Job. Research assistant."

"Find me an office and they will come," the guy said.

To which the redhead gave him a look that might have killed him.

"And how is it that job applicants magically appear?" she asked him.

"The flyer," I said. "At Ella's Place."

"Flyer at Ella's Place?" The redhead turned the killer stare at me.

"They weren't. She didn't. They were under the counter. I saw. I was. I really need the job." I took a deep breath. "So if you tell Dr. Silva. I'm available. For an interview." Jesus, Mary, and Joe, it was lucky that drool didn't come running out of my mouth.

The guy put a hand on my shoulder and said, real quiet, "She *is* Dr. Silva," which really made me feel like a friggin' idiot.

"Nick Silva? She's Nick Silva?"

"N-i-k, as in Nicola," the guy said.

"It's a mistake. My mistake. I'm mistaken. Sorry."

"She makes people nervous. But she's not so tough. I'm her brother, I ought to know. Billy." He held out his hand.

"I do not make people nervous," Nik Silva said.

"Ask her about Rusty's boat."

Nik sighed. "There is no job. Mr....?"

And here's where things got dicey. In

giving myself a new identity I forgot to give me a new name. Any self-respecting witness protection program will give you a new name and I sure as hell didn't want to use the old one. Nikki Silva was kind of staring at me again and my pulse rate was up around two hundred, so I spit out the first thing came into my head.

"Parker. Parker Bench." I wished, right after I said it, that I could have taken it back. I wished I'd have come up with something, anything, else: Jerry Lewis or Phillip Morris or Captain Crunch. Just about anything would have been better than Parker Bench.

Nikki raised her eyebrows. "Parker Bench?"

"It's a family name," I said, having to come up with some reason, quick, why I had such a dumb moniker.

"Well, like I said, Mr. Bench—"

"Call me Parker," I said, feeling I might as well get into it. And, to tell the truth, the new name did kind of calm me down a little.

"Like I was saying, Parker. There is no job."

"Yes, there is," Billy said.

"No, there isn't. I don't have enough money to pay me let alone a research assistant."

The rain started beating down on the metal roof of the storage room like the rhythm section of the band. I know that I should have let it go. But I was thinking about the day and how I didn't know where I could go to get out of the rain. So I stood there and mentioned Ella's Place again and how the flyer had said.

"I'm going to kill Ella right after I kill Jeremy," said Nik to her brother. "And then you're next. Consider yourself warned."

"Come on, Nik. The guy needs a job. At least give him an interview."

Nik closed her eyes and rubbed her forehead in the way my Nona used to when I did something stupid, like wash the cat in the tub. "Even if there were a job, he's hardly qualified. I can't just hire someone off the street."

Billy came over and put his hand on my shoulder. "Do you know anything about boats?"

"Yes. Yeah. Sure." Okay, the only time I'd spent around boats was fishing with my cousin Arnie in a rowboat we rented for the day on this little lake in South Jersey. What I learned was I should have put on sunscreen, and too much beer and a hot day can make you sick and probably keeps you from catching fish.

"See," said Billy. "Boat knowledge." Nik did that thing with her forehead again. "What about fish? Nik here is a fish doctor, you know. So you have to know something about fish."

"Sure, yeah, I know fish." Okay, about the only thing I knew from fish was how to make a nice bouillabaisse.

"See," said Billy. "Fish knowledge. What more could you want?"

"Billy, even if I could hire an assistant. Which I can't. I certainly can't hire somebody who walks in off the street. We don't know anything about this guy." She turned to me.

"With all due respect, Mr. Bench, Parker, I don't..." Nik just shook her head. Guess I couldn't blame her much.

"I'm a fisherman. Was. From Nova Scotia. That's Canada. I came here to find a job. Fishing."

"Fishing," repeated Nik, like she didn't quite believe it.

"Fishing," said Billy, taking my hand. I thought for a minute I was going to have to tell him all about Murray. Just to make sure that he knew I wasn't, you know, looking for companionship. Billy turned my hand over and ran his fingers over the calluses along my thumb and the pad of my palm. I worked hard to get those calluses, I'll tell you what. Any good chef worth his salt and paprika has them. I can pick up a steaming pot without flinching, no kidding. Billy pointed the calluses out to his sister. "Proof," he said.

Nik ran a finger over my palm. Jesus, Mary, and Joe, I wasn't near as calm as I'd thought. "I'll be damned," she said. "you have calluses just like... a fisherman."

I took my hand back. "Yes. I fisherman. Me. I fish."

"I still can't hire you, though."

"Nik," Billy began, but Nik held up a hand.

"It's nothing personal. It's just... There is no job. I have no money to hire an assistant." She looked at her brother. "And I'm not taking charity from Jeremy, so don't even start." Then back to me. "This isn't even my office. I don't have an office. So I'm sorry about the wild goose chase. Good luck in finding work. Summer's coming. I'm sure you'll find...something."

And with that she walked out of the room. I couldn't believe my luck or my lack of it. Woman of my dreams walks in to my life, then walks right back out again.

Chapter Thirteen

Nikki

I knew that, in his own way, Jeremy Fine was trying to help. And yes, he was doing it to worm his way into the good graces of the Silva clan, or at least to worm his way into my good graces which would, he must have supposed, eventually lead to his being embraced by Pop and Aunt Viddie. I was pretty sure this wasn't going to happen. And Jeremy, despite his best efforts, was not even close to meeting my needs.

What I needed was a real research project, with real assistants, a graduate student or two from Woods Hole who'd be willing to chum the waters for a chance at a name on a paper. That's what I'd had and lost thanks to Professor Gilmore and his whopping nerviness when it came to women. I'd driven the car over the toes of what I'd had and, to be perfectly honest, I'd do it again in a heartbeat. The fact that Gilmore never filed charges just proves he knew damned well he was flirting with disaster when he propositioned me.

All that aside, though, what I needed was to get back to where I'd been. I had a plan to do that. A simple plan. I'd get the Bay Commission to fund the study on dogfish populations, a study that has long been on the minds of conservation groups and commercial fishermen both. I'd do a bang up job with the study, which was a piece of proverbial cake as studies go, and use the good will I'd earn to sail my way back into the good will of the academic community. Who would eventually, or so I hoped, come to realize that worshipping at the altar of Harvey Gilmore was worshipping the Golden Calf, and a misogynistic Calf to boot.

Such was the stuff of dreams. The reality was that Ned wanted to give me the study grant about as much as he wanted a migraine, Senator McGowan was clueless when it came to anything having to do with the ocean save the eating of lobster, and I was stuck with a fairy godfather who offered up big purple pleasure cruisers, desks in T-shirt shop storage rooms, and flyers to which every wackadoo in Provincetown would respond. Not that I thought Parker Bench was a wackadoo. No, Parker Bench seemed lost and maybe a little confused and a whole lot desperate. And gorgeous. I know that isn't something you usually say about a man, but this guy could stop traffic.

My heart had been dancing around double time in theT-shirt shop and it had taken all my composure to tell him I had no job for him. It was hard looking into those great green eyes and telling him I couldn't help him. And I remembered where I'd seen him before because my heart had sprinted then too. He was the almost-certainly gay guy who'd been sitting on the bench at the pier

83

when Jeremy had shown me the boat. The man on the park bench. Parker Bench indeed. The guy was making it up as he went along, but I have to admit that he intrigued me.

I don't believe in magical thinking, but there I was stopped at the corner of Bradford and Conant in the driving rain thinking about Parker Bench and who should cross in front of me but the man himself.

He was walking into the wind and rain, his head pulled into the collar of his jacket. If I were asked to paint a portrait of misery incarnate, I would have painted him, hunched over, moving headlong into the storm.

I pulled to the curb and honked. He looked up and, not seeing me, pulled his head back into his makeshift carapace. I rolled down the passenger side window and shouted his name into the rain. Still he didn't turn. "Need a ride?" I said, coming up alongside of him.

He slid into the passenger seat. "Thanks," he said, looking straight ahead as I pulled out of the spot. His dark hair hung around his ears, rivulets of water running down his face like tears. I had this notion of running my fingers through his wet hair. Enough already, I told myself. I handed him a Dunkin Donuts napkin.

"Thanks," he said again, wiping his face.

"Where can I drop you?"

He kept staring out the window as though he hadn't heard. "Can I drop you somewhere?" I repeated.

"Sure."

"Where?" Again he seemed to ignore the question. Slightly agitated, I said "Where are you staying?"

"Staying?"

"Staying. Lodging. Spending the night. Hanging your hat."

"At. Um. The Inn."

"The Provincetown Inn?"

"That's it. The Provincetown Inn."

The Provincetown Inn was the most exclusive inn on the outer Cape. It hosted people like Senator McGowan and had even hosted the occasional foreign dignitary. So forgive me if I didn't quite believe that the likes of some seemingly homeless guy calling himself Parker Bench was staying there.

I called him on it. "No, you're not."

"I'm not? Why not?"

"Because folks staying there do not go walking in rainstorms without umbrellas."

"They don't?"

"And neither do they apply for jobs posted on flyers."

"I see." Parker pointed to the turn for McMillan Pier. "You could drop me off down there, I guess."

"Look," I said, as we splashed into the pier parking lot. "I'm sorry about the job."

He shrugged and with a sad smile said, "No harm. No foul," and opened the car door. "Thanks," he said again, and he looked at me with those great green eyes before getting out in the rain.

I know I should have left well enough alone, but I have this bad habit of not letting it lie. Poking the pit bull, my brothers call it. I watched as Parker sat at a picnic table under the awning on the deck of Moby Dick's Clam Shack, which was still shut up tight for the season. I wondered how long he'd sit there and went to sit next to him.

"A little damp for outdoor dining, don't you think?" I said.

Parker watched the rain waterfall from the eaves. "I love the rain, it's very wet."

"It is wet."

"Yup. Really soaking. Wet."

The wind changed direction and began to blow the rain onto the table. "Frankly, I think rain is better appreciated from a dry location."

"I like dry, too. It's a nice change from wet."

"Do you like coffee?" He looked at me curiously. "You know, hot beverage. Made from beans."

"I've been known to drink it."

"Are you aware that Ella's place has the best coffee in town?"

"Judging from the two cups I had this morning, I'd say that was probably true."

"Are you also aware that Ella is my sister-in-law and that I have free coffee status at her café?"

"You don't say."

"I'm pretty sure I can wrangle a cup for you."

"So, " said Parker, as we got back into the truck, "Ella is Billy's wife?"

"Not hardly. She's my brother Harry's wife."

Parker nodded thoughtfully. "I kind of

thought that Billy was, you know, gay."

"Billy is, you know, gay." I couldn't help smiling. "I thought that gaydar was a myth. But you guys do seem to have some sort of telepathy in spotting one another."

Parker's look went from thoughtful to pained, and I added. "I didn't mean to offend you. But you are gay, right?"

"Oh. Yes. Right. Gay as they come." Parker grimaced, as though the mention of his orientation was cause for gritted teeth and epic determination.

Aunt Viddie was the only person I knew who still wore curlers in public all day so that she can be well coiffed for an evening of watching TV. I spotted the tell-tale green curlers covered with a pink scarf as soon as we walked into Ella's place. Viddie, positioned to see and be seen, spotted us as well and waved cheerfully, before wresting her way out of the booth.

"You could have warned a person," I said to Ella, who was behind the counter.

"Oh, yeah. Viddie's here," said Ella. "You've been warned." Ella eyed Parker, a question mark in her eyebrows. "You were here this morning, right?"

Before Parker could answer, Viddie barreled over and grabbed my arm. "Nikki! Just the gal I want to see." I smiled and made ready to introduce Parker to both relatives, but before I could get a word out, Viddie said,

"You'll never guess my news!"

"Hmm..." I said. "Pope's coming to

town?"

"No, silly girl." Viddie slapped my arm. "Tripp's coming home!"

My cousin Tripp, Viddie's only child, was the apple of his mother's eye. He was a thirty year old bachelor who'd never kept a relationship or a job for longer than six months. Word had it that he'd lost his latest gig, at a garden center in Marshfield, because he was dumping the dregs of his Starbucks coffee into the unsold azalea bushes. He'd claimed to management that caffeine promoted plant growth, but apparently management hadn't seen it that way.

"He's going to come live at home for a while. Get back to his roots. You know. Just like you..." Viddie said.

"Yup," said Ella, "you and Tripp are two of kind, all right."

I gave her the stink eye. Viddie, still clutching at my arm said, "I think he'd be perfect for you."

"Excuse me?" I was, in no way, desperate enough to date my first cousin. I was in no way desperate enough to date Tripp Snow even if he hadn't been my first cousin.

"No, silly," said Viddie, catching, for once, her misstatement. "I meant for the job. As your assistant. Tripp has lots of experience in assisting, you know."

"I'm sure, but Viddie, there is no job."

"Of course there is." Viddie held up a pink flyer. "It says so right here."

"I was going to trash them," said Ella, ignoring the murderous look I was giving her and smiling.

"How much are you paying, dear?" asked Viddie. "Not that Tripp needs much. He can live with me. But, you know, what with car insurance. Will you offer Blue Cross? He's got that mole on his cheek. He really ought to have that looked into."

"Viddie," I took the flyer from her and folded it in half. Even as I did, I knew it was futile: I could proclaim no job until the seas dried up and Viddie would still ask that I hire Tripp. "I'm sorry, but I've already filled the position."

"So soon?"

I put my hand on Parker's arm. "I'd like you to meet my new assistant, Parker Bench."

Chapter Fourteen

Marco

You should have gotten a load of the face that Viddie made at the two of us, like she'd just been fed a spoonful of nasty and had to pretend it tasted sweet. It was nice to know that not all the crazy relatives in the world are related to me and living somewhere in the greater Trenton area. Nice to know, especially, that the unflappable and gorgeous Nik Silva had a few nuts in the family tree. Nik is a cool customer, though. When Viddie said, "Well then, isn't that fine?" and practically ran me over to get to the door, Nik had already found her way to the booth carrying two coffees.

"Don't mind her," she said.

"So," I said, "I'm your new assistant." Which almost got a rise out of her. She clattered the spoon around the cup a few times and looked kind of pained, just pained enough that I said, "Kidding. It's okay. I know from relatives."

I was going to tell her about my Uncle Albert, who swears to this day that he was captured by Indians when he was ten. The man has never been out of the Garden State, so far as I know. But I didn't want to give away too much, so I just kept my mouth shut.

She looked about ready to say something, when Ella came over with a piece of raspberry pie and set it down in front of me. "Celebrate your new position," she said. "It's on the house."

"Where's mine?" said Nik. To which Ella pointed to the counter and said that Nik could get it herself.

"Where you from?" said Ella, when I thanked her.

"Jersey," I said, without thinking. Nik had just come back with her own pie. "Born in Jersey, moved to Nova Scotia ten years back." I took a bite of pie so I wouldn't have to answer any more questions I might get wrong.

"Jersey to Canada, you do get around," said Nik, once Ella had left for the kitchen. I took another bite of pie.

"God, this is good," I said. Nik shook her head at me. I was pretty sure she didn't believe me about much of anything. But then again, she'd just hired me for a pretend job, so I figured we were about even.

We didn't mention the job again until she drove me back down to the pier. "I'm going to have to hire you," she said, parking the truck.

"You don't have to, I'll find something," I said, as much to reassure myself as her. It was still raining and blowing like a son of a gun and the idea of sitting it out under Moby Dick's awning wasn't so appealing.

"No, I have to. Because if I don't, Aunt Viddie will catch wind of it and then I'll have to hire Tripp. Even if I had a job available, I wouldn't want to hire Tripp."

"Well," I said, "I owe you for coffee and pie. That's about an hour's worth of work, what with tax and tip."

Nik looked at me and smiled. Jesus, Mary, and Joe, if they could bottle that... "Will work for food..." she said. She turned and looked out the window, the smile faded and she sat there for a long minute. "That's it! No, it's nuts, it'd never work."

"I'm game," I said.

"You haven't even heard what I have to say."

"I heard 'work for food.' I like food."

"Room and board," she said, looking at me again. "I could pay you in room and maybe, I do the shopping for me and Pop, I could throw in a few things and bring them. The *Queen* has a pretty nice galley," she was nodding, "and then I could talk to Ned again."

"Okay, right." I had no friggin' idea what she was talking about, but she looked so damned enthusiastic that I couldn't help feeling a little enthusiastic myself.

"Well, come on, then." She got out of the truck and I followed her down the pier to the strangest looking boat I'd ever laid eyes on. Even in the downpour I could see it was purple. Jesus and Mary, that boat screamed flamer. "The *P-town Queen*," said Nikki, heading down the gang plank.

"You own a big purple boat?"

"It's a loaner," she said.

"You borrowed a big purple boat?"

"Long story," she said, opening a door that lead downstairs—below decks—Nik would call it. Below decks the *Queen* outdid her shiny purple self. She had red leather chairs, a big red leather bar, and a pair of handcuffs hanging from the ceiling. Off to the side was a small bedroom (stateroom, according to Nik) with a huge bed topped in gold lame. The walls were papered in an interesting design. If you looked close enough, you could see them: tiny gay men doing what they would do if they had a big gold lame bed.

"She's got a good galley," said Nik, ignoring the wallpaper. She pointed to a kitchen just big enough for a stove and a half fridge. The cook top was new and the counter top, though limited, was new. Pink, but new all the same. "It's also got a good head," she said.

I wasn't sure I wanted to talk about that, what with the wallpaper, but Nik pointed out a small bathroom with a shower stall. Then she pointed out my clothes, and suggested, none too gently, that I make use of the facilities while she called the owner of the boat and fixed it so it became my new home.

I wasn't crazy about the idea of living on a floating gay emporium, but the shower, which had about the finest stream of hot water I've ever come across, made me change my mind. That shower was about the best I've ever taken. There were peach-scented soaps and little fancy shampoos in a mesh basket and I just about used them up.

The towels were purple, to match the boat, I guess. They were those big fluffy bath sheets that you can really appreciate if you've been drying off with paper towels.

I wrapped a towel around my waist thinking maybe the gay life wasn't so bad after all. These guys knew from comfort, I'd give them that. Nik was talking on the phone, her back to me, and I slipped into the stateroom and sat on the huge gold lame bed. The sheets underneath were soft and silky and it wasn't gay I was thinking. To be honest, I was having a little fantasy about Nik and those soft sheets and well, that was trouble, wasn't it? I told myself I better cut it out, because Nik was about as likely to lay down across those sheets as was Murray, my imaginary boyfriend. Then Nik knocked on the door. "Jeremy says it's fine if you stay here. He also said there are some clothes in the chest of drawers."

I checked it out. The only thing in the chest of drawers were a pair of black bike shorts and a pink silk shirt with ruffles that looked like it had been lifted from a gay pirate.

Chapter Fifteen

Nikki

To say Parker Bench cleaned up well would be an understatement. He walked out of the stateroom, freshly shaved, still damp from the shower, wearing a pair of Lycra bike shorts, looking like he belonged in a Bowflex ad. God, he was gorgeous and there was my heart, doing the tap dance again. I reminded myself that a lot of the guys who hang out at Spiritos Pizza late at night look like they spend half of their lives on a Bowflex. It's kind of a running joke among the locals: if he looks like a he could pose for a calendar, it's more than likely a gay calendar. Parker smelled like ripe peaches. He was carrying a blouse. Not a shirt, mind you, a blouse. "This is all I could find," he said, holding the suspect article out to me.

"Interesting find," I said, taking it from him and holding it up. "Looks like Jeremy raided the *Pirates of Penzance*."

"I can't wear this," he said, when I handed it back.

I'm aware that not all gay men are queens. Billy is a prime example. If you put a Miller in his hand and sit him on a bar stool down at the local tavern, you'd be hard pressed to tell him from any of the other fishermen who'd come in for a brew. But this was P-town, a guy could walk down Commercial Street wearing a tiara and chaps and no one would blink. In fact, there was a guy working at the Stop & Shop deli who did wear a tiara and chaps.

Parker looked dubious, but he put on the blouse and started to button. Truth was, he looked better without the shirt and I'm pretty sure the gay population of my town would have agreed with me there, but, as I pointed out to Parker, the Stop & Shop did have rules, as in: "no shirt no shoes no service." Frilly blouses and tutus optional.

Still, it must be said that Parker did not look comfortable in his new role as pink pirate at the Stop & Shop and, to add to our troubles, Aunt Viddie was holding cousin Tripp hostage over near the olive counter, no doubt having him sample the Kalamatas to make sure they were up to his highly honed standards. I dragged Parker over to frozen foods as quickly as I could, but alas, it was too late. Tripp had caught our scent and, in a valiant effort to escape his mother, had tracked us down.

"Well, hello there, fair cousin." Tripp made an exaggerated bow just as Viddie came plowing down the aisle. "Been kidnapped by pirates, have we?"

"That's her new assistant." Viddie smiled as though one of the curlers still on her head had dug into her skull.

"No kidding?" said Tripp. "Just come from the Seven Seas, have you, matey?"

"Just come from Scribbs," I said, smiling. "Undergrad at Harvard. Scribbs for graduate work, did a little time in Woods Hole. When I needed an assistant, he's the first guy I thought of. Called him this morning."

"Is that so?"

"Yes." Parker nodded thoughtfully. "I've been in Canada. Studying—"

"The effects of climate change on the cod population," I said breezily.

"Well, cod," said Viddie. "One of Tripp's favorites, isn't it? I'm going to make some tonight with asparagus. You should try the asparagus, it's fresh. Grown right here on the Cape, in Truro."

"That sounds swell." I looked at my watch. "Oh golly, we're going to be late, Parker."

"Late?" he asked.

"For the costume party. Get a bunch of oceanographers together at a costume party, you just don't know what's going to happen, isn't that so, Parker?"

"Oh, sure," said Parker. "They're a barrel of fun. Those crazy research bastards."

I steered Parker to the checkout line, where I paid for the one package of Elio's frozen pizza we'd plunked into the cart.

"This the party food?" Parker held out the package once we'd climbed into the safety of the truck. "That's board."

"This is not board. I know beggars can't be choosers and all, but us oceanographers can't live on frozen pizza."

"They can. But not to worry. I'll take you to the Dairy Queen."

"In this?" he said, pointing to his outfit.

"This is P-town," I said. "They'll probably think that you're applying for assistant manager."

Parker sighed deeply. "Again, beggars can't be choosers, but would it be possible to get some real clothes?"

I hadn't considered that hiring a homeless guy would mean getting him properly outfitted. But, given the glowing resume I'd just given Viddie and Tripp, Parker had a point. I had twenty dollars in my pocket and a credit card that was nearly maxed out. Lucky for me that research folks weren't known as fashion plates. "Good thing I didn't give you a law degree," I said.

Chapter Sixteen

Marco

"Get whatever you want," she said, but I could see by the way she was shifting back and forth on her heels that what she meant was "as long as it's under ten bucks." So I perused the menu posted up over the Dairy Queen counter carefully and ended up with a hot dog and some onion rings. She got herself a tall glass of ice water, which confirmed my suspicions that she wasn't exactly swimming in dough.

"I ate at home," she said, when she caught me looking at the empty place mat in front of her. She waved at a kid taking out the garbage. "My nephew Linc," she said.

"You related to everybody in this town?" I asked. I was kind of kidding, but it sure did seem that way. I'd never lived in a place as small as P-town and for all I knew, incest ran rampant in the dune lands.

"Nope. Just half," she said, stirring a straw through the ice water. "Other half is gay." With this she gave me one of those looks, meant to make me quit asking questions, which made me remember to be humiliated by the way I was dressed. And also to remind me that I was supposed to be gay and that I was going to have to be a great actor, considering what her stare was doing.

I smiled at her and said, "My kind of people," and raised my eyebrows to make a joke of it.

"Wait until summer," she said. "You'll have more dates than you know what to do with."

That wasn't something I wanted to consider. "I'm not looking for dates," I blurted. To which Nik raised her eyebrows, real curious and not in a jokey way.

"There's someone. This guy. Murray. In Canada. Murray. The fisherman." I was about to start drooling again.

"Murray, the gay Canadian fisherman?" Her tongue was doing this little tango inside her cheek and I could pretty much tell that she was going to ask a lot of questions.

So I quick said, "Bet there's a lot of tourists here. In summer?"

Nikki was no fool and it was pretty clear that she knew exactly what I was doing. But she went along with it anyway. "Oh yeah. You can hardly move around here between Memorial Day and Labor Day. Place is wall-to-wall with the tourist trade."

"Tourist trade," I said, my mind gone to a little place on the beach or maybe on the pier. Little place with outdoor tables and strolling musicians... And that line of thinking took me to Roma's and Vlad the Impaler's head resting in a bed of gnocchi, which made me shudder.

"You afraid of tourists?" Nikki asked. I smiled and offered up an onion ring, which she took and dipped in ketchup, then pointed at me. "Bet Murray the gay Canadian fisherman isn't afraid of tourists."

After dinner, we went to the Army & Navy store on Commercial Street. The place smelled like no place else I've ever been: a mix of dust and old and some weird kind of incense and rubber. Not a bad smell exactly, though it took a little getting used to. We walked past a display of pinwheels and a barrel full of gas masks to a rack of shirts that looked like they'd been hanging there since the Korean War.

As I started looking through the stuff, I noticed that Nik had started that heel dance again, same as she had when I was deciding between clam strips and burgers at the Dairy Queen. I saw her glance more than once at the price tags.

A kid came over to ask if we needed help.

"Pants, Ford. We need pants," said Nik, after introducing the kid as her nephew Ford. Swear to God, I was going to need a chart to keep all her relatives straight.

"We got those gray Dickies Dad wears on the boat." Ford led us to a wall of workpants neatly stacked and sorted by size.

"About a thirty-six?" Nikki eyed the bike shorts and reminded me once again of why I needed new clothes.

"Thirty-six long," I said, wanting to get the whole business over with.

"Fourteen ninety-five," said the kid, Ford.

"Not bad." Nikki took three pairs of

identical gray pants. She unfolded a pair and held them out to me. "Try these," she said.

I was reminded of my Nona and the shopping trips we took to Sears when I was a kid. She always made me get these tough skin pants, which were nowhere near as fashionable as the jeans I wanted, and could outlive a nuclear attack. A lot like the pants Nik handed to me.

"Perfect," she said, when I came out from behind the curtain wearing them. Though the kid, who didn't have a lot of fashion sense judging from the boxers hanging out around the back of his cargo pants, did not nod in agreement.

"We'll take them." Nik handed Ford the other two pairs. She picked out three blue work shirts, twelve ninety-five a pop, to match. Back behind the curtain I went to change into one of them. I thought about just leaving the pink shirt for some other poor schmuck to find, but since it was borrowed, I scooped it up with the bike shorts and went to the counter, where Ford was running Nikki's MasterCard through the register.

"Uh, Nik," he said, a pained look on his face. He whispered something to her.

"Oh, crap." Nikki took one pair of pants and put them back on the shelf. Ford rang us up again and shook his head. Nik went from crap to shit and put back a shirt.

By the time the card went through, shit had become fuck and the only clothes we bought were the ones on my back.

"I can wash my other clothes at the Laundromat," I said as we left the store. "It'll be fine."

"I don't want to talk about it," she said, climbing into the truck.

"I'm just saying, I'm used to making do. Don't worry."

"What part of 'don't talk' do you not understand?" asked Nik.

Chapter Seventeen

Nikki

The absolutely worst part of living in a small town where you're related to half the population is that the minute something goes wrong, like say a boat blows up or your credit card is maxed out, everybody knows. Ford went home and told Ella, who spent the next morning trying hard not to pry into my finances. "Do you always buy clothes for your assistants?" she asked.

"It was a loan. I was just going to loan him some clothes money."

"Jesus, you'd think somebody with a Harvard education could buy his own pants," she said, pouring me another cup of coffee. "But then again, Viddie might have got the facts wrong."

"No," I said, "Harvard it is."

"Right." Ella poured herself a cup of coffee and plopped down in the booth across from me. "He must of graduated the year before me. I was so busy, what with being crowned Queen of England and all, that I just missed him entirely."

"Okay, so he's not a Harvard grad," I said, sipping my coffee. By the way Ella was looking at me, I knew that I'd have to come clean sooner or later. "Okay, he's a fisherman. From Nova Scotia."

"So you hired a fisherman to do research?"

"I had to. It was either that or hire Tripp."

"He is better looking than Tripp, I'll give you that."

"He's gay."

"You hired a gay Canadian fisherman." Ella pointed her spoon at me. "That's too bad, because you need to get laid."

"I've become celibate," I told her. "Men are way too much trouble." Ella gave me a pained look, put the spoon in her coffee, and started to stir, slowly. "What, you got a problem with celibacy?" I asked.

"Something Viddie told me," said Ella.

"You talked to Viddie about getting laid?"

Ella didn't crack a smile. "Father Marini is retiring."

"That's okay," I said, "I wasn't going to sleep with him."

"They've named his replacement," said Ella, ignoring my comment. She gave me a hard stare. "Local guy," she said.

"Shit." I put down my cup, the coffee sloshing over the edge and staining the paper placemat.

"So I hope you're serious about the celibacy thing. Because you can't sleep with him, either."

I had slept with Eli Avellar, but that was long before he became Father Eli Avellar, the ordained priest. My brothers ribbed me that I had chased Eli to celibacy. On a particularly bad day, I could almost believe that. Eli was my first love. And on a good day, I knew I was his. As for Eli's walk with God, well, the truth is that it began, as far as I knew, long after Eli and I had gone our separate ways. And we had parted ways nearly twenty years ago. I hadn't seen him since.

When I went out to the *Queen* later that morning, Jeremy was on deck, talking with both hands, while Parker nodded.

"I see you two have met," I said, handing Parker a cup of coffee and a muffin from Ella's.

"Your new cabin boy is charming," Jeremy said. Parker blushed, mumbled something about a grocery list, and escaped below decks.

"He is pretty," said Jeremy, "if I was not totally committed to your baby brother."

"But you are," I said, "totally committed."

Jeremy put his arm around my shoulder. "Did Kate Smith belt out 'God Bless America?'" he said. He gave my arm a squeeze. "Now, I don't want you to fret your sweet rust-colored curls, but I may need the *Queen* back."

"What?" I asked, drawing away from him.

"It would be temporary, darling. Just for a few days." He let go my arm and gave me a sidelong glance. "Aren't you going to ask why?'

"Okay. Why?"

Jeremy threw both arms into the air. "Antonio Verdi!"

"Who is Antonio Verdi?"

"Who is Antonio Verdi? Who is Antonio Verdi? Antonio Verdi is the greatest chef this side of the Atlantic, darling. Tuscan cook extraordinaire. He is going to put the Red Tomato on the lips of every Zagat guide reader on the East Coast!"

"He's going to cook for you? At the Tomato?"

"That's what he's coming to talk to us about. Billy and I have the tiny condo and it just won't do to have the great Antonio sleep on the couch. So I thought to myself, self I said, why not let him stay aboard the *Queen*? What better way to impress a man of such renown? He arrives next week. Dear God, it would be glorious if he could cook for us. His clams casino are To. Die. For. An orgasmic experience."

Parker came above deck just as Jeremy was expounding on orgasmic experience. "Much like your cabin boy!" finished Jeremy, making Parker blush again.

"No more than a few days," said Jeremy. "Now I really need to run. Ciao, bambinis!" He blew an exaggerated kiss Parker's way and sashayed off the boat.

"Wow," said Parker.

"He's engaged to my brother," I said, just in case Parker were having any thoughts of dumping his gay fisherman boyfriend.

"Well, too bad for me, huh?" said Parker, although he didn't look like it was too bad. In fact, I'd have to say he looked downright relieved.

Chapter Eighteen

Marco

I learned that first week on the *Queen* that witness self-protection is about as good an idea as self-surgery. Six days and I was living on pizza and hot dogs, spending my days on a big purple boat. Nikki foraged through her brother Pete's closet for some cast off work clothes, which would have been fine except that Pete outweighed me by about twenty pounds. So Nikki goes and finds this discarded belt with a silver buckle that's about the size of a small state. Another cast off, and it wasn't any wonder.

And, speaking of fine, Jeremy Fine dropped by the boat once or twice every day to chat me up. He was some piece of work, that guy. He actually went so far as to invite me out to what he called the cove beach. To watch the wild boys, he said, then he went on to tell me it was the best way to get laid. Which meant I had to give him my spiel about Murray. After which he'd come by and ask if I'd heard from the old ball and chain.

Worse, he starts teasing Billy about being the ball and chain. And Nik's little brother Billy is a stand-up guy. The kind of stand-up guy that, if I may, in my humble opinion, deserved better than a flirty queen like Jeremy. I tell you, if I'd really been gay, I would have gone for a guy like Billy. Didn't hurt that he was the spitting image of his big sister.

Which of course leads right back to the toughest part of the self-witness protection act: Nikki Silva. Who spent most of the week pacing up and down the deck with a cell phone pressed to her ear. No, let me rephrase. She spent that week shouting into the cell phone pressed to her ear. When, finally, she shouted, "I can't catch anything but a cold sitting on this damned boat," the guy at the other end must have had enough. Because she snapped the phone shut, said "Have a nice day, you asshole," and pitched the phone off into the harbor. Woman has a hell of an arm, let me tell you.

Like a fool I went and asked if it was bad news. She gave me a look that could make dogs howl.

"I'm getting a stipend," she said.

"Stipend? That's money, right?" I couldn't see how that could be bad news. The stipend got me to thinking about the Stop & Shop and real food. The galley on the boat was decent enough, and with a little fresh asparagus and some white fish just off the boat, I could cook up a decent meal for once.

"That's charity," said Nikki. "Or a bribe. Take your pick."

I should have known to leave well enough alone, but I got to go and remind her that she'd promised me a trip to the Stop & Shop.

"Problem with the cuisine?" she said. And if the thought of another can of beans wouldn't have sent me overboard, I would have let it go. "As a matter of fact," I said. "The cuisine could be better."

The produce at the Stop & Shop wasn't what you'd call first rate. The tomatoes were of the hot house variety that looked better than they tasted. But if you were careful, there were some good buys. The asparagus, for one, was grown local. And they had a decent olive bar. I got a couple tomatoes, some fresh basil and a lemon, along with cod, which Jason at the fish counter swore had been flopping around on a boat deck a few hours before. To this I added some milk and some cream and some butter. All the while Nikki watched as though she couldn't figure out what I was doing.

"I take it you can cook?" she asked as I was sorting through the parsley, most of which looked like yesterday's leftovers.

I found a bunch that wasn't so bad, and not wanting to let on too much about my past, I told her that I liked those cooking shows on TV. After that Nikki stopped asking questions, though her stopping had nothing to do with cooking shows. She was staring at the deli counter and from the look of her, I half expected to see Viddie over there ordering a pound of ham. But when I turned to have a look, it wasn't Viddie at all but two men, both of them wearing clerical collars.

"Trouble with the Lord?" I asked.

"You might say that," said Nikki as the

younger of the two men turned and, seeing Nikki, froze over by the salad bar, the two of them, Nik and the priest, staring at each other like they'd both seen ghosts.

"Shit," said Nikki, breaking the silence after what seemed like a couple of years passed by. She started thumping a cantaloupe. Beating on a cantaloupe is more like it. When I tried to take it from her, she dropped it into the cart. On top of the eggs, no less.

"What is wrong with you?" I said, though it was pretty obvious. The priests, both of them, were on their way over to the produce section.

Nikki stepped closer to me, so close that I could smell the lemon shampoo in her hair. Made it hard remember the gay thing. So hard that, without even thinking twice, I put my arm around her waist.

The younger priest caught sight of us then and gave me a look that the pope wouldn't have approved of, like he was going to set me on fire.

"Nikki," he said. "How are you?"

Nikki leaned into me and said, "Eli, I heard you were in town."

To which the priest looked around like maybe she's talking to somebody else. "I'm back," he said. "Both of us, back. Imagine that."

Then Nikki mumbled something about being on our way and started shoving me and the cart towards the checkout. And me, I realized that I still had my arm around her. Which I removed in a hurry and in the interest of witness self-protection by way of being gay, I started rubbing it, pretending I got stung by a bee.

"I can't be buying gourmet food," said Nikki, as she threw the groceries into the back of the truck. "If you want this stuff, you'll need a second job."

"One that pays money, you mean?" I said, grabbing the bag with the eggs in it so that at least a few of them would be spared.

Chapter Nineteen

Nikki

My run in with Eli at the grocery store convinced me of one thing: I was going to have to get the study done. I was going to have to get the study done so that I could get a real job. In Hawaii, maybe. Or Alaska. Or anywhere as far away from New England as I could get.

After a lot more groveling and crow eating, Ned had agreed to give me a stipend. After paying the money due on my credit card, the stipend money would be just enough to keep my truck from getting repossessed. As for the grant, the only thing I heard from Ned was, "Be patient," and "the senator's looking into it." I knew stonewalling when I heard it, and Ned was stonewalling big time.

It occurred to me, though, on the way back to the *Queen* that I might get a handle on the study without grant money. I had a boat, after all. And an assistant. All I needed was some equipment. Who was I kidding? I had a big purple pleasure boat and an assistant who, when I explained the Lincoln Index, a way of counting wild life populations that I intended to use for the dogfish count, said, "I knew honest Abe was smart, but don't that beat all." I'm not sure if he was kidding. I hope to hell he was. Even as we were carrying the groceries on board the *Queen*, he was telling me he couldn't imagine that counting was all that hard. Then he began chanting "One, one little fishy, two, two little fishies, three, three little fishies, ha ha ha" in a bad imitation of the Count on Sesame Street.

"Are you about done?" I asked, once the annoyance factor had gotten completely out of hand.

"I am done," said Jeremy Fine, who had apparently been lurking below decks. Again. "Done in, done over, done well and often," he added, eying the bag Parker was carrying. Jeremy was spending altogether too much time on the boat and I had a sneaking suspicion that he was doing it to watch Parker's back. Or, more to the point, to leer at Parker's butt. The very thought made me want to spit nails. Jeremy was, after all, supposed to be committed to my baby brother. And though all he'd thrown Parker's way thus far was a little flirtation and a lot of looking, I had to wonder how far he'd go if Parker didn't have the good sense to keep him at arm's length.

At that moment, though, Parker's physique was not the center of Jeremy's attention. In fact, Parker could probably have danced naked while juggling the tomatoes we'd bought and Jeremy wouldn't have done much more than bat an appreciative eye.

"May I present Antonio Verdi," said Jeremy with a flourish. A smallish man dressed in a black cape had come up behind Jeremy. He looked so much like the Count on

Sesame Street, whom Parker had just been imitating, that I had trouble hiding a smirk. Parker, for his part, had actually turned his head and was pretending to admire a seagull sitting on one of the pilings.

Pop always maintained that the measure of a man could be taken by how firmly he shook your hand, so my second impression of Antonio Verdi was that Pop would not have been impressed. Chef Verdi's handshake had all the vigor and firmness of a wet Handi Wipe.

"Antonio the Great has come to save the Red Tomato from certain mediocrity," declared Jeremy, nearly dancing around the caped chef.

"No kidding," I said. Parker had taken both bags of groceries and disappeared below deck.

"Indeed, madame," said the great one himself. "I am chef at L'Ecole des Poissons. I'm sure you've heard of it."

I hadn't heard of it. I did remember from rudimentary high school French that l' ecole meant school and I entertained a vision of Antonio the Great, cape in place, as a cafeteria lunch lady. It became harder not to smirk after that. Not that Jeremy or Antonio would have noticed, the mutual admiration society had left the deck and gone below.

I don't know what prompted me to follow. I could have just stayed where I was. But, as my brother Pete often reminded me, I seem to have a morbid curiosity when it comes to predatory behavior and these two had the feel of big fish about them. Big fish about to take a chunk out of a little fish in the guise of Parker Bench. Not that I thought Parker was entirely defenseless. It was just that, as gay men go, Parker seemed a little out of place.

I came below deck in time to catch the great one sniffing at the bags Parker was unpacking. "The asparagus might do," said the chef. "As for this," he held up the parsley with two fingers as though he'd just pulled it from a dumpster, "this is a horror. This is the stuff of nightmares."

I grabbed the parsley from him. The great one ignored me, having settled on rooting through bag number two. He sniffed the cod and declared it passable.

"Stop pawing our dinner," I grabbed the cod and put it back in the bag. Parker, looking a little peaked, followed my lead as we began repacking the bags. "Parker and I were planning dinner on the boat," I said, making it up as I went along. "We have a lot to discuss about the study."

"Better to study them than to eat them," said Jeremy, in a poor attempt at humor. "But I'm afraid that the boat is otherwise engaged."

"You said Tuesday. Today is Monday," I said, reminding Jeremy, that, when I'd pressed him, he had given me a date for Antonio Verdi's arrival. As it happened, my brothers were planning a few days on George's Bank and Pete had offered up his room as a place for Parker to crash for the night. Tomorrow. Tonight, I'd have to scramble to find lodging for my assistant.

"Tuesday, Monday," said Jeremy. "What is time?"

"Time is we agreed on tomorrow," I said. But it appeared that the great one had had a dent in his schedule and thought a little R&R on the Cape would be just the thing to revive his flagging spirits. And, since Jeremy owned the boat, there was not a thing I could do about it.

Parker and I did, to our credit, manage to hang on to both bags of groceries despite broad hints from Jeremy that the great one might be able to turn his mojo on it and provide a feast not only for Jeremy himself, but also for Billy, who would be swinging by after returning from Boston, where he was talking to a restaurant supplier.

Parker mumbled something about the great what's his name stinking as much as three day old fish as we put the groceries back into the truck.

"Good thing it's a nice night," he said, "because I'm going to have to sleep in the truck bed."

"You have food. Don't be an ingrate," I said. Though I was at a loss as to where Parker might spend the night. I thought about Ella's, but her house was already packed with people. And Pete's place was a single room with a hot plate, a dorm-sized refrigerator, a pull-out couch, and a large screen TV, which constituted all of Pete's possessions since his divorce. With Pete at home, there was barely room for him, let alone company. I could have berthed Parker on the *Two Sons*, Pete and Harry's boat, but the two of them were leaving at high tide, dawn tomorrow, and I thought better of it.

So it was either Pete and Harry and Billy's old room, across from mine under the eaves at Pop's house, or the back of the truck. I would have chosen the truck bed had it been a little warmer.

"I should warn you about my father," I said, as we pulled into the drive. "He can be a little touchy. And he's a little weird about the whole gay thing."

Parker thought for a minute. "We don't have to mention it," he said, "the gay thing. I mean, if it's going to make life difficult." I began to wonder just how difficult being gay had made life for Parker Bench. Enough so that he was willing to keep secrets. Given the made up name and the boyfriend that I was pretty sure didn't exist and the whole Canada by way of New Jersey thing, I would have said Parker had quite a few secrets and maybe, since I hadn't yet unwrapped the real Parker Bench, he was pretty good at keeping them, too.

"That might be for the best," I said, feeling kind of angry at myself for saying it. Parker was gay, my better angels said, and Pop would just have to deal with it. But the lesser angels all agreed that maybe it was good to leave well enough alone.

Pop was asleep in the Barca Lounger, the remote in his lap. The TV was tuned to the History Channel, a documentary about the Battle of the Bulge. Which was an improvement over QVC anyway. He woke up, as he always did, when I took the remote and turned off the set.

"Company, Pop," I said. My father opened a single eye with which to examine Parker, trying, I'm sure, to decide whether or not company was worth both eyes. "My new research assistant, Parker Bench," I said. "He brought dinner." I knew that the dinner part would probably decide in favor of Parker.

"What kind of dinner?" Pop opened the second eye.

"Cod, sir," said Parker.

"You plan on fixing it?" asked Pop. "Because this one here can't cook to save her life."

Parker might have been nervous around Pop at first, but once he hit the kitchen, all nervousness dropped away. It was kind of strange, watching him take charge. Kind of arousing, too, to watch him wield a knife with such expertise. I imagined taking the knife from him and unbuttoning his shirt. Crazy, I know. I chalked it up to transference because I was still a little undone by my run-in with Eli.

"Is this the sharpest knife you have?" Parker ran his hand along the blade. I pulled out the knife sharpener and changed the subject back to the study, explaining statistical analysis to Parker as he chopped garlic and threw it into hot oil in the pan.

The TV was on again, Pop watching something with canned laughter, but the garlic soon lured him to the kitchen. He came in just as I was accusing Parker of not hearing a word I'd said.

"Garlic?" asked Pop, sticking a finger into the Kalamata olives that Parker had chopped.

"Yes, sir." Parker tossed a few of the olives into the pan with the fish and gave the whole thing a turn. "Cod ala Parker."

I set out plates and Parker put the food on them. Pop took a cursory bite. "Where did you learn to cook, boy?"

"Food Channel," Parker said.

"No kidding," Pop took another bite then pointed his fork at me. "You ought to tune in to some of them shows." He turned the fork on Parker.

"You're good. You could cook at my kid's place."

"You mean the Red Tomato?" asked Parker.

"The 'in the red' Tomato, more like it," said Pop. "God only knows what Billy's got himself into. I pray for him every day."

I wasn't sure whether or not Pop was referring to Billy's business venture or his relationship with Jeremy. The next thing he said made his line of thought pretty clear. "Not that I don't live and let live, mind you. Oh, it's a sin, true enough, but what with the AIDS and all, you got to feel a little pity. Just that my own boy, I keep hoping he'll see what's what." Maybe it was the food, but that was more than Pop had said on the subject since Billy came out.

Food, or the bottle of red wine Pop pulled out for dinner, or that Parker was about as unassuming as they come, the fact was my father took to Parker Bench like a sand flea takes to sand. By the time we'd finished the last of the wine, Pop had told at least a dozen stories about his days with Uncle Ed on the *Two Sons*, detailed his plans for the garden he plants every year, which, really, is little more than a tomato plant and a few peppers nestled in a weed patch, and shared a recipe for fisherman's stew my mom used to make.

By the time we got to after-dinner coffee, Pop was ready to invite Parker to live with us permanently.

"It's a good sized room, got a triple bunk that we bought for the boys when they were kids, but I'll have to clear her out," he said, as the three of us headed up the stairs. The room was the larger of two upstairs bedrooms and was across a small hall from the room that had been mine and was now again mine, with a small bathroom between the two. Since the house, an antique Cape, lacked an attic, the boys' room had been used for storage since Billy moved out of it some five years ago. I hadn't been in the room in years and storage was a bit of an understatement. The room was, in fact, filled with boxes.

Pop cleared a way to the old bunk bed saying that it would be just fine with him if Parker wanted to move some of the boxes out.

I opened a box behind the door. Inside were a set of three sponges, three chamois wipes, and three smaller sponges, all of them still wrapped. "What are these?" I asked, holding up a chamois.

"That cloth holds fifty percent more water than your ordinary sponge," said Pop. "Just soaks it right up. And, if that weren't enough, it's got wax and detergent built right in." I dropped the sponge back into the box and noticed a shipping label.

"Fort Lauderdale?" I read aloud. Then it hit me. "Please don't tell me it cost nineteen ninety-five."

Pop took the box from me and stacked it with some others. "So what if it did? This is a useful item. I was going to give it to Pete and Harry for the *Two Sons*. Plus I got three sets of sponges for the price of one."

The sponges were just the tip of the iceberg. Pop had also acquired a garden shower, a portable sewing machine for buttons only, and three extra large bottles of something called 'Grease Off,' and those were just the boxes near the door.

"You," I said, trying to be as firm with Pop as he'd been with us when we were kids, "have got to stop watching late night TV."

"Oh, for the love of Mary. It's a few things. Useful things, I might add."

I pointed the leather-punching tool that I'd unearthed at him. "Pop, this isn't a few useful things; this is a warehouse full of junk."

Parker had begun stacking boxes to one side. "The stuff might have some resale value," he said. "Like on Craig's List. Or you could do a garage sale."

"Or a flea market!" said Pop. "You hear that, little girl? I could take it over to Wellfleet. Make a killing."

"What do you know about flea markets, Pop?"

"I can learn what I need. Dora Cook has a table over there. She can tell me what's what."

I supposed that the flea market wasn't a bad idea. At least, we'd be rid of the clutter. But a killing? There was a reason, I told Pop, that the stuff wasn't sold in stores. To which he said that I ought to take a page from my new assistant and get a more positive attitude.

By the time we'd cleared a space and found sheets for the bottom bunk, Pop and Parker were planning a trip to the Wellfleet flea market, which Pop was pretty sure would lead to a late-life career as a flea market entrepreneur. I'd never have said it to Pop, but he sounded an awful lot like Billy before one of his big enterprises. Like the ill-advised Red Tomato, which is what had gotten us here in the first place. Memorial Day was less a month away, and though Jeremy was lining up a chef and redoing the kitchen, the dining room still had a partially collapsed roof. Which could, in my humble opinion, make it tough to open. Butmaybe Pop was right.

Maybe there was power in positive thinking.

All of the enthusiasm over flea markets had served to give me an idea about the research I was proposing: I needed equipment, which was expensive. But maybe, just maybe, I could get used equipment. And, by keeping expenses to a minimum, maybe, just maybe, I could get funding. I got up early the next morning and began making a list of what I needed. Pop, who is always up early, had some great ideas on where I might get things like netting and line.

Parker was clearly not a morning person. He stumbled down the stairs in boxers and a T-shirt, his hair sticking up every which way, at 9:00 a.m., hours after my list was done and Pop had brewed a second pot of coffee. Parker poured some coffee, mumbled something about shaving, and stumbled over to the bathroom.

Pop, who would have been perturbed had any of his own children stumbled into the kitchen after having slept through the most productive part of the day, smiled after him. "That's a good looking fella," said Pop. "And don't tell me you haven't noticed."

It wasn't the first time that Pop had tried, in his own way, to find me a fella. He'd said the same of the UPS guy who delivered the many packages that had ended up in storage upstairs. He'd also mentioned, at the time, how UPS is a fine company that takes good care of its employees. None too subtle, was Pop. And I was not about to have any of it.

"He's gay," I told him.

Pop's mug of coffee stopped halfway to his mouth. He put it down.

"That's not so."

"It is so. Ask him yourself."

"It's not so. He don't look it."

"Sure he does. You just got all carried away because he can cook."

"Now listen to yourself. Plenty of men cook. Doesn't make them gay."

"He's gay, Pop. He told me so."

"Nah," Pop looked at the mug. "Really?"

"Yep. Gay as rainbow pride."

"Oh Lord. I asked him to be my business partner." I shot him a look as he fingered the rim of his coffee cup. "After you went to bed. We talked about the flea market thing. He had some good ideas. And since you're not paying him..."

"He said I wasn't paying him?"

"Not like that. He explained about the funding and the room and board. He wants to help you out with the ..." Pop looked at me. "Oh Lord. What if folks get the wrong idea? About being partners?"

I couldn't help snorting. "Pop," I said, "You couldn't be gay if you wanted to."

"Sure I could," said Pop. "It just so happens that I don't want to."

Chapter Twenty

Marco

Sometimes you got to wonder at fate. About how you can get onto a bus going someplace you've never been and find out that maybe it was the place you were heading all along. I'd been in P-town a couple of weeks and I felt as though I'd lived here all my life. And, more than that, that I *could* live here all my life. A lot of that had to do with Nikki. She had a temper, sure, but she was beautiful and smart. And her old man was a great guy. The kind of guy who would give you a fair shake.

I ran the razor over my cheek and let my mind wander to an imaginary house up the street. A little place for Nikki and myself, where we would plant a garden and every Sunday we'd have Nikki's pop over for dinner. And every Saturday all summer I'd go with him to the flea market. And I'd do all the cooking and Nikki could do her research and maybe we'd get a dog.

I cut my chin in the middle of the fantasy and the blood brought me back to what was real. I was pretending to be a gay fisherman named Parker Bench. I was deceiving Nikki and her father and when they found out, if they found out, any hope of a

127

rose-covered cottage off Bradford Street would be dust. And if they didn't find out, I was stuck with being a gay fisherman with an imaginary Canadian boyfriend.

Still, I had to make the best of things and it didn't hurt that I got on swell with Pop Silva. Only, when I came back to the kitchen, ready to make some omelets like we'd talked about, the ones with linguica sausage in them, Nick muttered something about having had breakfast hours ago, and went off into the living room and turned on the TV. I was stunned. "Did I do something?" I asked Nikki.

"That's just Pop being Pop."

"But last night..." I said, "We were talking about the flea market. He was so great. I don't get it."

"I told him you were gay."

"Why? Why would you say something like that?"

"Because you're gay."

"Well, okay. So what if I am? Why did you tell him if you knew he'd get all upset?"

"Parker," said Nikki, putting a hand on my shoulder, "he was going to find out sooner or later."

I wasn't ready to let go of the whole dream. Not yet. "I've got to talk to him," I said.

Nick Silva was sitting in his Barca Lounger, paging through a Burpee seed catalog.

"Those big boys are great," I said, as though he'd never walked out of the kitchen. "They make a marinara that's to die for. You grow those, I'll make you enough sauce to freeze. Last you all winter."

Nick turned the page like I wasn't even there. I began flirting with the idea of telling him the truth. Maybe offering to marry his daughter once I got a divorce from Lark. Then I thought of Vlad the Impaler lying in a pool of gnocchi and I decided that the truth wasn't such a hot idea.

"I'm sorry I'm gay," I said.

That, at least, got Nick to look up from the catalog. It gave me a little hope. And an idea. "I've been trying to reconcile," I said. Nick put the catalog down. "I'm pretty religious," I said.

"That so?"

"I know it's a sin and I'm trying to change it. Change my. You know. Orientation." I took a deep breath. Might as well go for it; I had nothing to lose, right? "There was this group," I said, "back in Canada. They think that you can shake it with prayer. The gay thing. Like AA kind of, the group. One of those twelve step programs."

Nick furrowed his brow. "You don't want to be gay?"

"I am, though. Gay, I mean. But I think I can, you know, keep it under control. Like with the group."

"Gay-aholics anonymous?" I looked over to see Nikki standing in the door.

"This is serious," I said, trying hard to sell it. "You know, faith can help."

"Help with what? Becoming un-gay?" Nikki's eyebrows shot up.

"People change, little girl," said Nick Silva. "Look at Eli Avellar."

"Eli is not and never was gay," Nikki

said.

"But he changed." Nick pointed a finger at his daughter. "He got a calling. Who's to say a poor boy like Parker couldn't have a conversion or something. Happens, you know."

"We are not having this conversation," said Nikki, shaking a finger right back at her father before stomping back towards the kitchen.

"You really think you can do it?" asked Nick.

"Sure," I said, then thinking that maybe I shouldn't be so sure, I added, "Well, maybe. I need help, I guess.

"Well, son," said Nick. "I suppose we all could do with some help now and again."

It took a week for Jeremy Fine to sweet talk Antonio Verdi into cooking for the Red Tomato. I'd of bet that Antonio didn't know a ladle from a sauté pan, but maybe I was just jealous. The guy was a major league douche and Jeremy was all but walking behind him on his knees so he could kiss his ass whenever Antonio stopped to bend over. Billy told me that Jeremy had offered the great one a six figure salary and Billy wasn't exactly what you'd call pleased about that, either. I would've bet he didn't like Verdi any better than I did.

All the while, Nikki was gathering up fishing line and calling to yell at Ned, her ex-husband. Although I'd never met the man, I figured him for another big douche. Which also might have been jealousy. Though the way Nikki talked about him, it was pretty obvious that she'd have liked to throw him to the sharks herself.

I got to say, though, living at Nikki and Nick's was a damn sight better than living on the *Queen*. Now that I'd made a pledge to reform, Nick and I were back to being pals. We even joked about Viddie, who, a couple of days after I'd started sleeping at the Silvas', came over to announce that Tripp had gotten a job. A good job. A job that was a damn sight better than anything Nikki had to offer. Nick and I were moving boxes into the garage at the time to get ready for the Wellfleet flea market.

"Doing what?" Nick had asked, barely looking at her.

"Manager of a Shoppe," said Viddie. Swear to God, you could hear the e at the end of shop the way she said it. "Little boutique down off of Commercial Street. Brand new place called Good Vibrations."

"Good Vibrations, huh?" Nick shook his head.

"Little place sells beach toys. Get it? Beach Boys, Beach Toys. I think it's very clever. They have boutiques in Boston and New York and they think Provincetown is the perfect location for a new Shoppe, what with the beaches and all." Viddie looked very pleased with herself. So pleased that, after she walked off, Nick said that by the looks of her you'd of thought she got a new job.

"Dollar to donuts he doesn't last the summer in that Shoppe," said Nick, emphasizing the e.

And so it went for the better part of the week, with me and Nick taking inventory, listing contents and prices, figuring out a good strategy for the flea market, since Nick had too much for one table. I suggested that we do the whole shebang over three weeks' time, and Nick liked the idea. He said, in fact, that if the flea market thing took off, he'd buy more stuff to sell. I was kind of glad Nikki wasn't around to hear that.

Anyway, things were going just fine, me working, cooking for Nick and Nikki, and feeling pretty good about the whole deal, when Nick announces on a Tuesday night that he's set up an appointment with Eli Avellar over at St. Peter's.

"There's no group," Nick said, "But Eli does counseling and he's happy to take you on."

The only time I'd met Eli was that one time in the store with Nikki, and judging by the look he gave me then, I was pretty sure he'd just as soon murder me as counsel me. But since I'd promised, I was stuck between the old rock and the old hard place and so on Wednesday night, off I went to St. Peter's rectory and knocked on the door.

Truth was, I had nothing to be scared of. Father Avellar and I were about the same age and he was a really good host, offering me tea and cookies. We sat in his office, and he took a chair next to mine instead of behind the desk and sat there like we were just going to have a friendly conversation.

The other truth was that I was scared. Maybe not so much scared as intimidated, I guess you'd say. Like I've said, my Nona who raised me was a really good Catholic, Mass every Sunday, no meat on Friday, the whole nine yards. She tried real hard to make me a good Catholic. I'd been an altar boy, for God sake. Which is why I sat there in a cold sweat staring at Father Avellar's collar and thinking that if I lie to this guy, any and all chances of getting through the pearly gates are good as gone. 'Course, I wasn't sure there were any pearly gates to speak of, but who wants to take those kind of chances?

"I'm not gay," I said.

To which Father Avellar, who'd said I should call him Eli, furled his eyebrows. "Denying it isn't going to make it go away, you know. Frankly, I think it would be better if you got comfortable with your orientation. Though don't tell the pope I said that, okay?"

"Sure, yeah, but you see," then I thought about who he might tell. He knew Nikki pretty well and last thing I needed was for word to get out. "This is like confession, right? Anything I say is just between you and me?"

"I won't tell if you won't," said Eli, smiling at me. And so I told him, the whole truth and nothing but. When I got through, Father Eli had quit smiling.

Chapter Twenty One

Nikki

I was not thrilled with the idea of Eli counseling Parker and not only because I didn't believe in conversion. I was thirty-six and I'd dated plenty of men over the years. But the list of those who mattered was pretty short. Eli Avellar was on the top of that short list. And because he was, I wanted to stay as far away from him as I possibly could, given the constraints of a small town that was surrounded by water on three sides. With any luck at all, I could get the grant money for the study and I could spend my days out on the *P-town Queen* doing the research I was meant to be doing. The ocean was a big place, with plenty of room for staying away from old hurts and memories.

The problem was, of course, that Ned was the one holding the grant money purse and Ned was second on the list of those men who had mattered. The fact that Ned could still provoke me enough to chuck my cell phone into the Atlantic probably said a lot about my state of mind. I spent half the time wanting to kill Ned and the other half wanting to ravage him. The problem with that was, I'd thought I was through with the big Swede who'd first been my research partner and then became my husband.

When I think about how easily Ned walked away from both of those things, it makes me want to feed him to the sharks piece by bloody piece. Because he had walked away from research and marriage as though neither counted for much of anything. He'd come back to the channel island from a trip to the mainland one day and asked how I felt about moving back east. I thought it was just a theoretical discussion. Sure, I told him, someday. Maybe. I loved my father and my brothers, went back a couple of times a year to see them. But I'd lived in California since college. And Ned had grown up in San Diego. We had work to do there.

Then Ned told me he'd taken a job with the Massachusetts Bay Commission. Not that he was considering a job. Not that the job had been offered and he was toying with the idea, but that he'd taken the job. I had, up until that point, no idea the job even existed.

Ned argued that he was getting too old to swim around with sharks and live in isolation on an island. I told him that he was crazy to want a bullshit sit-behind-the-desk job and that I wanted nothing to do with it. I loved our island, loved the rock-crashing surf, the bellowing sea lions that sunned themselves on the beach. I loved Ned, in part at least, because his passion for this life, this work, reflected my own. We would spend hours free diving to watch hammer sharks swim in formation, hours waiting for a white shark to feed on a seal carcass we'd hung over the side of our boat. I wanted that life, had worked hard for it, and until the fateful day that Ned came home to tell me he wanted something different, I would have bet Ned loved it too.

I pushed hard to make him stay. I should have known, after five years, that pushing Ned only served to strengthen his resolve. Still I pushed. In my darker moments I think that it was my fault, that I pushed him to an ultimatum. Choose, I said, me or the East Coast bullshit job. He chose the East. It was hard for me to forgive him that. Hard, even after he left, to imagine that the man I'd loved had been replaced by someone I didn't know or understand.

After he left, I lived alone on the tiny channel island, trying to put it all into perspective. In the end, it always came down to the work. I loved my work. If solitude was the price I had to pay, then so be it.

Then Harvey Gilmore cut my funding and I ended up doing the one thing I'd told Ned I would never do. I moved back home. The irony was not lost on me.

And there I was, living with my father and the newly acquired mystery man, Parker Bench. There I was, calling Ned and nearly begging him for money. And being told that I'd have to be patient. Patience, I have to admit, has never been my strong suit.

But I waited, trying to figure out ways around the money, e-mailing everyone I knew, until some two weeks after the *Queen* had been taken over by Antonio Verdi. Who, in an aside, seemed in no hurry to get back to his chef-dom at the famed L'Ecole des Poissons. But just when you think it's done for, just when the flea market business starts looking like a lucrative idea after all, something happens. In my case, it was a call from an old friend, Mary Rider. We'd been lab partners at UC San Diego. I'd gone on to the Channel Islands and she'd gone to Florida, where she was still doing research in conjunction with Florida State.

"I heard it through the grapevine that you need tracking equipment," she said

I could barely believe my good fortune. Then I remembered the lack of funds. I explained the situation to Mary.

"You could borrow. I could maybe get them to delay payment. For a few months anyway."

Mary, I knew, was putting her rear on the line here. The equipment was, even used, expensive, and borrowing wasn't something of which the bean counters at Florida State were likely to take a kindly view. "Harvey Gilmore is a pig," said Mary. "I think you got hosed and I'm just doing my part to see that justice is served." She went on to tell me how Dr. Gilmore had once spent an entire evening with his drunken hand brushing her thigh. "I wish I'd have had the guts to run him over," she said.

We trashed Gilmore for a while and talked of old times and eventually got back to the slightly dated, slightly used equipment.

"You are my personal Santa," I said.

"Don't get too excited. You are going to

have to pay eventually."

I told her where to send the stuff. Then, on a whim, I told her that she could just bill the commission.

I knew that the bill would make Ned morph from rock-mode to storm-mode. I figured a little rise in blood pressure would do him a world of good.

Chapter Twenty Two

Marco

It felt pretty damned good to tell the truth to someone, though I got to admit that Eli Avellar might not have been the best man to talk to. Oh, I knew he was a priest and I'd have bet good money even then that he wasn't the kind of guy who took his vows lightly. I'd laid a pretty heavy burden on him, though, and by the look of it, it wasn't going to be an easy thing for him to keep my secret. I don't know what I would have done had the situation been reversed. It was pretty obvious that it was all the man could do not to get burned by the torch he was carrying for Nikki Silva. At least that's what I thought at the time. I thought, that's the one thing we had in common, we both had a hard time figuring out where Nik was supposed to fit into our lives.

Of course he advised me to come clean with the Silvas and of course I told him I couldn't. I told him that if Phil was on my tail, the worst thing I could do was get the Silvas involved.

"But you have involved them," Eli said.

"First sign of trouble, I make like the wind," I told him.

"How long do you suppose you can

keep running?" asked Eli. He had a point. I could travel from here to China and back again and nothing would be solved.

"He might never find me anyway," I said. "Long as I stay here and try and be gay."

"I don't know if I can go along with this charade," Eli said.

In the end he did go along with it. He wasn't happy about it, but that was neither here nor there. Bottom line was that he cared about Nik and her family and that he was a decent guy. I came by every Wednesday. Eli taught me to play chess. He trounced me bad those first few weeks. But I'm a quick study, and by the time the Chef left town, some three weeks after he breezed in, with a contract to cook in a restaurant that still didn't exist, I captured Eli's queen. Which was not the same thing as capturing his trust. Or Nikki's heart, for that matter.

Nikki by then had a pile of equipment and a boat to use it on. To say she was itching to go out to sea was an understatement. I, on the other hand, was in no great hurry. I'd learned a few things about fishing by hanging around with the Silvas. It was easy to get Nick talking; all I had to do was mention something about netting and his eyes would glaze over and he'd be off on some tale or another. To fake boat knowledge while actually out on a boat would be a lot harder, I knew that. Like or not, the day was coming when Nik and I would take the *Queen* out for a spin. I knew that, too.

There was nothing for it; I helped her load her equipment on the boat. I didn't know the half of what I was unpacking, not that Nik cared if I did. I couldn't for the life of me see how all those gizmos could make anyone's eyes light up, but Nik's did, every time we cut our way into a new package.

"You know what we need?" she said, plugging a couple of batteries into a computer.

"A nice glass of Chard?" I said.

"More rope," she said, not even smiling. She sent me over to Rusty's marina. I came back down the pier with the rope slung over my shoulder, looking like a guy in an Old Spice ad, when I caught sight of Nik on board with a tall blond man. Had to be her ex-husband. A man I'd started calling Thor after Nik had described him to me. There was Nik, flailing her arms and making me think we'd have to inventory whatever she'd pitched overboard. Then Thor grabs her shoulders with both hands, like he's about to throw her overboard or at least shake the life out of her, which made me start walking down the pier a little faster. I ran nearly all the way up the gang plank only to find the two of them necking like a couple of teenagers.

Which almost, but not quite, made me back down the gang plank. I dropped the rope and let out a cough instead.

Chapter Twenty Three

Nikki

What is it about Ned that made me that kind of crazy? I had no real explanation for my behavior on the boat that day. I couldn't explain it to myself and I certainly couldn't explain it to Parker. Not that I owed Parker, a man with more secrets than a CIA operative, an explanation.

I didn't give him one. His staged cough, a loud sputter that ended in an "ahem," threw an ice cube on whatever it was that had heated between Ned and me. I was, at that moment, sorry and chagrined. Later, after Ned said something to Parker about sharks not having the nerve to bite me because I'd have bitten them back, and saying to me that I'd better think twice about what I was doing. Later, after Ned had left the boat and I'd taken the coil of rope from Parker. After Parker had gone aft without saying three words to me, I began to wonder if there was any way at all to justify my actions.

It was the invoice from Florida that had sent Ned running, much as I knew it would. He'd driven the hundred twenty miles from his comfortable home in Brookline just to climb aboard the *Queen* and wave that invoice in my face.

"What the hell?" he yelled, the paper flapping in the strong north wind.

I took the invoice, folded it, and put it in his jacket pocket, and very calmly told him that it was a hell of a deal. That new equipment would have cost twice as much.

"I said be patient. I said the grant money is coming. But can you listen? Stupid question. Nik Silva only hears what she wants to hear."

"Ned Anderson used to give a damn," I said, feeling my calm fly off on the strong breeze.

"I do give a damn," Ned said. "Why do you think I'm here?"

"Oh, you give a damn all right. You care deeply about your political connections and what they can do for you. You care about some big house on Chestnut Hill that buxom Beverly's big shot mommy's going to make sure you get for doing her bidding."

"Shut up, Nikki."

I had him at shut up. Furthermore, I knew that I had him at shut up. But whatever it is that gets my jets heated does not cool easily. "You aren't half the man you used to be," I said.

"Maybe I've grown up," he answered.

"Bullshit. You've grown away."

"There's a right way to do things, Nik. Look around you. Looks to me like you haven't made the best choices."

That was below the belt and a little too close to the truth for comfort.

"Why do you want to stop this research?"

"I don't. As I've told you, there is currently no funding."

"It's not a billion dollars, Ned. I'm asking for a pittance. I could make this run on the amount that Senator McGowan spends on a pair of shoes and you know it. Yet you keep me on some stipend that wouldn't pay for chum."

"Why can't you be patient?" Ned grabbed my shoulders and then it happened. The way it always happened when we fought.

"Patience is a virtue I don't possess," I said. "I figured you'd have known that by now." We crashed into each other and who knows where that might have led if Parker hadn't come along with a bad case of fake bronchitis.

The fact remains that Parker had happened along and that I was both embarrassed and miffed. Embarrassed that I had fallen into Ned's arms yet again and miffed that Parker had witnessed the whole thing. I threw the rope to the deck and, knowing full well that Parker was lurking somewhere below, I went down to where I'd stacked boxes and began setting up the computers.

I was hoping that Parker, who would clearly be of no help in this endeavor, would just go away. No such luck. He came out of the stateroom and watched as I set up the GPS.

"Billy told me there's no way the Tomato will be ready for Memorial Day. Jeremy's kind of bent about it, I guess," he said, so completely changing the subject that I felt an urge to throw my arms around him and thank him.

"Yeah, you kind of need a restaurant to run a restaurant," I said.

"Is the place that bad?"

"Bad would be an improvement," I said, and I went on to describe the caved-in roof and the squirrels that had set up housekeeping in one corner of the dining room.

"Jeremy wants to get the kitchen squared first. Billy says they want it state of the art. He's right that you need a good kitchen."

"You've been hanging around with Billy a lot, haven't you?" I said. I didn't mean to pry, but it was clear that the two of them got on well. Billy had a way of bringing out the ease in people. Parker did too. The two of them seemed a good fit.

"Billy's good people," said Parker, coloring a little.

"But you're spoken for," I said. "How is Murray?" I couldn't help myself, I loved needling Parker about Murray the Canadian fisherman, a man who probably only existed in fairy tales. "When's he coming to P-town?"

Parker shrugged. "I don't know. Someday soon."

I rolled my eyes. "Caught up the Maritimes, is he? I think you like Billy. I think you like him a lot."

"There's nothing there, Nik. Billy's heart belongs to Jeremy."

"I love my baby brother, but he's not such a great judge of character when it comes to choosing life partners," I ventured.

"Must run in the family," said Parker.

Chapter Twenty Four

Marco

Nikki didn't take the bait and I didn't push. Because, really, it was none of my business. Really, if she wanted to wreck her life with a lug like Thor then so be it. I had no right to come in and try to change it. Much as I liked P-town and much as the Silvas had become like family, much as my heart bounced around every time Nikki so much as glanced in my direction, I was an outsider. I was temporary. Maybe, I started thinking, it would be good to leave now, before I got myself in too deep. I had started thinking about Canada. Maybe I could make it go, maybe open up a good Italian restaurant up there. They had cities in Nova Scotia, right? And towns, places with tourists who would pay good money to eat on the patio of a little trattoria set out on the harbor of some little fishing town. I could have wrought iron tables and green umbrellas with chairs to match.

I could quit P-town. Soon. Soon as I'd helped Nick Silva set up his flea market business. Soon as Nikki was done counting her fish. Soon as the Red Tomato was up and running.

Not that I believed the Red Tomato

would ever be up and running. If ever there was a restaurant doomed to fail, it was that one. It made me shake my head, the way Jeremy went about doing business and the way that Billy, who if you asked me was the brains of the two, let him do it. Made me feel a little sorry for Billy, to tell the truth. He was a stand-up guy and he was way too good for the likes of Jeremy Fine. Almost made me wish I was gay. Because Nikki was right, I would be a much better partner for Billy, if I do say so myself. I wouldn't run around looking at other men and kissing the ass of every two-bit chef that happened along, that's for damned sure. And hell, I could make that restaurant work. Forget Antonio Verdi, that guy didn't know Parmesan from Romano. I could make something of the Tomato.

But, like his sister, Billy had the right to make his own decisions. Who was I to interfere? I should just go, I thought again. I should just tell them all Murray missed me and I should leave.

But then Nick Silva bought a Louis the XV bedroom set on eBay and I knew someone had to stay to keep an eye on things.

It was delivered the same day that Nik had her little get together with Thor. They, whoever had brought the thing on the truck, had left it on the Silvas' front lawn: One king size headboard padded in white, two huge dressers, also white, with gold gilded hardware, one mirror that looked like the one Snow White's stepmother used, and two matching gold-plated lamps. Nik swore under her breath when she got out of the truck and went to confront her father. The two of them started howling at each other and I began to think that maybe, just maybe, I'd been sent here for a reason. Blessed are the peacemakers, right? At least that's what Sister Immaculata over at Sacred Heart Parish School used to tell us.

Though when Nikki gave me the hairy eyeball and said, "Look what you've started," I began to think that Sister Immaculata may have been a little off in the advice department and that peacemaking was highly overrated.

"Me?" I said.

"This isn't Parker's doing," Nick said.

"I thought we agreed, Pop. No more stuff. You've got enough to keep you at the flea market all summer as it is."

"That's small potatoes, little girl. This," Nick waved a hand towards the lawn, "is money waiting to be made."

"How much did you pay for all this?" said Nikki, imitating the hand gesture.

"Doesn't matter. I've already found a buyer," Nick said. Nikki let out an exasperated sigh and turned the eyeball on her father. "Not that it's any of your concern, little girl, but it just so happens that Viddie is very interested in buying a new bedroom set for Tripp."

"Viddie??" Nikki asked.

"Yes, Viddie. She's coming over to look at it this very afternoon."

"And how do you propose to get it to Viddie's? Tie it to your back and hump it over?"

"You've got a truck. I'm sure you'd be kind enough to let me borrow it."

"I've got a small truck. You need a moving van."

"So we'll make a couple of trips. Parker can help me tomorrow."

"It's going to rain tomorrow. And besides, I'm starting my project tomorrow and Parker is going to help me."

"Parker's my partner," Nick said.

"He's my assistant," Nikki said. They had each grabbed onto one of my arms, pulling one way then the other. Much as I liked being popular, Canada was looking real good.

"Cut it out," I told them both, which got them to stop pulling but not to stop yelling.

"What are you going to do in the meantime, leave that mess on the lawn?" Nikki asked.

"I have a garage."

"Maybe we can postpone the shark thing," I said. It wasn't so much a peace-making move as a way to postpone my having to go out on the boat. But why not kill two birds with one stone, so to speak?

"Good idea," Nick said.

"No," Nikki said.

"Why not? You waited this long. Another day isn't going to kill you. And besides, you said yourself there's a nor'easter brewing."

"No," Nik said. "Verdi's coming back this weekend, which means he'll get the boat. And, besides, the blood won't keep."

"Blood?" I asked, swallowing a bad feeling.

Nikki jumped into the truck bed and

opened the storage chest. Inside were about half a dozen gallon-sized jars of red liquid and a large garbage bag. A rancid smell filled the air.

"What is that?" asked Nick, covering his nose.

"Sheep's blood," said Nik. "I have another shipment coming in tomorrow."

"And you're worried about eBay?" Nick asked.

I pointed to the bag. "That the sheep?" I asked.

"Seal," said Nik. "The carcass washed up in Boston. Max Groper procured it for me. It was a very lucky find."

"Wonder what he'll do for your birthday," I said.

"It was damned nice of him to save it for me," said Nik. "You can't let a thing like that go to waste."

Chapter Twenty Five

Nikki

Seals and sea lions are the shark version of filet mignon. Hang a seal carcass over the side of the boat, chum the water with blood, and it's like ringing a shark dinner bell. I was, as I told Pop and Parker, very lucky to get the seal. You can't exactly buy them in the meat department at the Stop & Shop. Max Groper, at least, is savvy enough to know this. As for the sheep's blood, I special ordered it from a meat-processing plant. That a rare carcass was available on the same day that the blood arrived was nothing short of providential. Pop and Parker could wrinkle their noses all they wanted. I was going to do this damned study.

I can't tell you how important the study had become. It began as a way to repair my somewhat damaged reputation, sure. But the more Ned stonewalled and told me to sit on my hands and wait, the more waiting for even one more day became agonizing. I entertained a fantasy of laying the completed study on his desk and saying that I'd done it. No thanks to him or his commission, I'd done it.

I was not about to let my plans get waylaid by minutia. Or by a Louis the XV bedroom set, which Aunt Viddie had come up the driveway to investigate.

"This is it?" she asked, as though maybe we had another few dressers stashed in the bushes.

"Yep," Pop patted the headboard as though he'd carved it himself. Aunt Viddie wrinkled her nose. "This stuff smells fishy."

"Nothing fishy about it," said Pop. "The smell hasn't got anything to do with the furniture. Your niece over there is hauling seal carcasses hither and yon."

"Seal carcasses? What in the name of heaven are you doing with seal carcasses?" asked Aunt Viddie, turning her wrinkled nose to me.

"Shark bait," I said.

"You and those gosh-awful beasts, I swear," said Aunt Viddie. "You're going to ruin your truck with that smell."

True enough that the truck bed might smell for a while. But I'd just wash the chest with vinegar and baking soda and leave the top open a few days. Besides, I'd grown used to the smell of chum over the years. Considering that she'd grown up in a family of fishermen, you'd think that Viddie was used to it, too.

"She's taking Parker tomorrow," said Pop. "So I can't deliver the goods."

"Why don't you ask Harry and Pete to help you? They're home for a couple of days. The Cars could pitch in, too," I said.

"Cars have school, the two of them," said Pop. "Pete's gone over to Hyannis to visit that waitress he's been seeing. And Harry won't help on account of me and Ella aren't speaking."

"Since when?" I ventured.

"Since yesterday when I went to the coffee shop and she told me that I should quit trying to help Billy."

Pop had been helping Billy by making broad suggestions that he, like Parker, ought to get Eli to counsel him. "Ella's right, you know," I said.

"She is not. And don't you start."

I rolled my eyes. "I'll go talk to Harry," I said. "I'm sure that you and Ella can mend fences."

"I don't know," Viddie said.

"You see," said Pop. "Viddie agrees that Ella ought to apologize."

"Not that," said Viddie. "I don't know about the bedroom set."

"What's the matter with the bedroom set? You said you loved Louis the XV." Pop said.

"It's awful big," Viddie said.

"Course it's big. It's fit for a king. It's supposed to be big," Pop said.

"It's huge," said Viddie. "I don't think it'll fit into Tripp's old room, what with all the pieces."

"Fine," said Pop. "That's just fine. Tell you what, I'll take it to the flea market come Saturday and make twice the money you would have given me. All of you are driving me nuts anyway what with your complaints and your seal carcasses and you're telling me how to treat my own kids."

"I almost forgot," Viddie shouted after

Pop as he stormed towards the garage, "Tripp's Shoppe is having a grand opening next week. You're all invited. They're having oysters and everything."

"Drive me nuts, with your Shoppe and your oysters," said Pop, going inside.

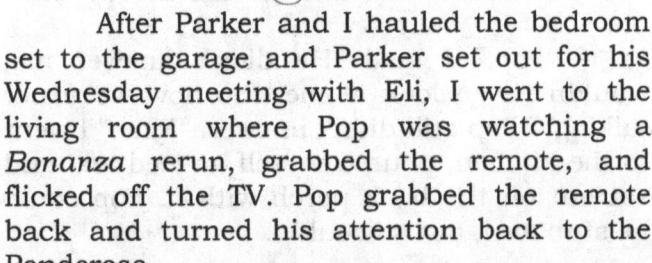

After Parker and I hauled the bedroom set to the garage and Parker set out for his Wednesday meeting with Eli, I went to the living room where Pop was watching a *Bonanza* rerun, grabbed the remote, and flicked off the TV. Pop grabbed the remote back and turned his attention back to the Ponderosa.

"Ella doesn't have to apologize for speaking her mind, you know," I said.

"Two peas in a pod," muttered Pop.

"What was that?" I'd grabbed the remote again, my finger on the button.

"You and Ella. Two peas in a pod. Now give me my clicker."

"You have to tell her you're sorry," I said, not giving the clicker back.

"Me? Why should I be sorry?" Pop took the clicker from me and shut off the TV. "You listen to me. I'm trying to fix my kid."

"You can't fix what isn't broken."

"Look at Parker. He's fixing it."

"Parker just wants you to like him. Though God knows why."

"Parker is changing. I know it. You'd know it too if you had eyes. He's a damned sight better than that Anderson character anyway."

"Parker is gay, Pop. So is Billy. That's a fact and no confessions or Acts of Contrition are going to change that fact."

"You're wrong, little girl. You and Ella both."

"No we're not."

"You got no faith at all. None at all." Pop shook his head and turned the TV back on.

"Pop," I said. He didn't answer me, wouldn't even look at me. "So now we're not talking?" Pop still didn't answer. "Fine." I went to the kitchen, poured myself an iced tea, and sat out on the back porch with it. Pop could be stubborn, but so could I.

Still determined to get out onto the Bank and test the equipment, I woke Parker at 5:00 a.m. He was still half asleep when we drove to the pier and, if it hadn't been for the seal carcass, he might have slept through the entire expedition. "God Almighty," he said, as I opened the chest, "it's gotten worse."

"Help me move it to the boat," I said, ignoring the interesting shade of pale that Parker's skin had become and the coffee he'd spit over the side of the truck bed.

"You want me to touch it?"

I tossed him a pair of heavy, rubber work gloves. "It's bagged. It won't bite you."

"It's a decomposing seal," he said, tossing the rest of his coffee over the side of the truck and throwing down the cup. "Who knows what kind of icky you can get from a decomposing seal?"

156

"Icky? Is that a new disease?"

Parker gave me an exasperated look. "Yes. It's in the medical journal. You can look it up. Under I."

I pulled on the gloves and began pulling out the seal. It weighed maybe fifty pounds, but it was fifty pounds of dead weight so I had a little trouble with it. Parker sighed in a way to match his look, pulled on his gloves, and took one end. "You sure we have to do this?" he said, as we lifted the carcass onto the *Queen.*

"Hell no," I said, going back for the blood. "I just love watching you turn green is all."

I gathered the rest of the blood, already collected and waiting at the boat office and, by six o'clock we were ready to sail. By 6:15, after Parker had given the pilings on the pier a few fender-bender type taps and nearly taken out a buoy, I took over steering the boat. I also began to wonder if Parker had lied about boat experience the way he'd lied about other things or if, as my brothers alleged about the hapless Rusty Cook, I made Parker nervous. Parker was, in point of fact, nervous the whole trip out to the Bank.

We would do the research at Stellwagen Bank, a marine life sanctuary some three miles from P-town. When we reached the edge of the Bank, I slowed the boat and gave Parker his first lesson in shark baiting. We hung the carcass over the stern. I turned on the fish-finder and steered towards the spot where several local fisherman had reported dogfish activity.

Dogfish activity isn't hard to spot. The sharks hunt in packs, hence the name, and they leave behind a trail of carnage that would make Attila the Hun proud. We soon hit upon the trail, bits of fish and blood. Up ahead I could see churning in the water. I handed Parker a pail, shoved a ladle in, and demonstrated how to ladle the blood around the carcass.

"This is disgusting," he said, taking the ladle from me. He was looking a little green again.

"If you're going to blow chunks," I said, "do it over the side. It adds to the stew." This, as I remember, was pretty much word-for-word what either I or Ned always told queasy first-timers. I know it sounds silly, but saying it again made me feel a little wistful. Parker did look like he was going to blow, but I have to hand it to him. He took a deep breath and after a few minutes, began to look like he'd been chumming his whole life.

Our first shark was a four-footer. We hauled her onto the deck, where she began thrashing and biting at the air. As would I, I suppose, if someone had forced me onto an alien vessel. Parker looked at the shark as though we'd just pulled her out of the depths of hell.

I handed him the tag gun. "Put it through the dorsal fin," I said, pointing to the spot where we needed to put the chip that would allow us to keep track of the animal.

"You've got to be kidding," he said.

"You might as well get used to doing it," I said. "It's not that hard. Now hurry up so we can get her back in the water."

Parker handed me the tag gun. "I quit," he said. "This job sucks."

"Come on. Consider it a challenge. You're not afraid of a challenge, are you?"

Parker took the gun. I should have warned him about the barbs. In truth, I hadn't given them much thought. I was used to working with people who actually knew something about sharks. Who would have known enough to stay clear of the barbs near the shark's tail. The barb caught Parker on the thumb.

"Shit," he said, dropping the tag gun.

Dogfish barbs are poisonous. Not seriously 'I'll kill you poisonous' in the way of a cobra bite, but bad enough to cause some pain and, if left untreated, make you sick. I grabbed his thumb, grabbed my knife, and made an x-shaped incision. Then I took his thumb and began sucking on the wound.

Parker barely had time to register any of this, but, as I had his thumb in my mouth, there was this moment, this tiny little glance on his part. If I hadn't of known better, I would have sworn he wanted me. In the way Ned had wanted me. The thought of Parker's lips on my neck shivered through my head. And the thought was not unappealing. For one tiny moment, until I came to my senses and thought that Parker would much rather kiss Billy than me, I wanted to seize Parker by those muscular shoulders and taste those full lips of his. And the moment passed and I spit the venom on the deck.

Chapter Twenty Six

Marco

As I've mentioned before, I've had a few romantic-type encounters in my day. Most of them were your run-of-the-mill garden-variety type of encounters. A few, I guess I'd have to say, were maybe just a shade this side of kinky, like this waitress that liked to take the ice out of her drink and put it in her mouth and go down on me. But, I got to say, having my thumb stabbed and then sucked by Nikki Silva was about the wildest thing had ever happened to me. Father Jesus, it was like being hit by the thunderbolt all over again.

My heart was doing double time in my throat and if I'd let things farther south determine my actions, I would have grabbed both sides of Nik's face and kissed the hell out of her. Maybe it was only me imagining it, but in that one second where she had my thumb in her mouth I swear to God if I'd have done what I wanted, she would have thanked me for it. Then she spit on the deck.

"Poison," she said, and for the next minute I thought maybe that was a comment on what had, or had not, happened on the deck of the boat.

Of course, Nik went on to tell me that

the barbs were poisonous. "So you saved my life," I said.

"Not hardly," she said. "Saved you from a big throbbing hand, maybe."

"Well, thanks." Now that the moment had passed it was replaced by a kind of awkwardness I wouldn't have wished on anybody. I wanted, after that, more than anything to impress upon Nik Silva that I wasn't the world's biggest fool. So after she threw the beastly poison-barbed fish back over board, I went back to chumming without being told. I tagged the next shark and the one after that. By the time we got to the sixth and last of our quarry, I was tagging like an old pro without getting stung.

Chapter Twenty Seven

Nikki

We tagged six animals that day. Parker was a quick study, as anyone who'd been barbed would be. His hand, though a little red around the puncture wound, was none the worse for wear. It was a good day all in all. The GPS tracking system worked like a charm and by the time we left the Bank, all six sharks were bleeping on my screen. That was the good news.

The bad news was that there was indeed a nor'easter blowing in and by the time we left Stellwagen, dark clouds had begun skulking along the horizon line, ready to mug us. Halfway into port the wind picked up and the bay began to pitch a fit, ten foot swells tossing the *Queen* like a teenager at a rave. We cut what was left of the seal and I pushed the engine as fast as I dared. It took all of my concentration to keep the *Queen's* prow to the swells, but I'd seen worse and, when the squalls and the swells didn't get any bigger, I was confident that I could bring us in without having to call the Coast Guard.

Parker didn't seem so sure. The pitching made him sick and I guess it didn't help that the chum bucket was sloshing and spilling on the deck. He held onto the rail, puked over the side, and announced to the ocean that he was not ready to die.

"You are not going to die," I told him. I had to shout over the wind, which Parker took as evidence that I was losing it.

"Oh, God," he said, before heaving again. "Hail Mary full of grace."

"Stop that," I said.

"There's blood all over the deck. The sea is boiling. I'm pretty sure it's the End of Days."

"Maybe you'll get carried to Heaven in the Rapture."

Parker was not amused. He puked again, on the deck this time.

"Toss the chum overboard," I suggested.

"Isn't it too late for that?"

"The Four Horsemen will appreciate the effort," I said.

"You can be a little insensitive, you know that?"

"I leave sensitivity to guys like you. Gays are known for their sensitivity."

"I'm not gay," said Parker, looking even more miserable.

"Right," I said, "Eli's a miracle worker and I'm Queen of the Mermaids." I don't know why I was so irritated at Parker and Eli. The truth was I was irritated with myself for having allowed a foolish thought about Parker to cross my brain. I was a star at picking out the wrong men.

First Eli, then Ned. In between and after a dozen or so shipwrecks that left me feeling ragged. And now I was harboring fantasies about a gay guy. Ella was right. I needed to get laid. Soon it would be summer and somewhere among the tourist crowd, with any luck, would be a dumb hunk of a straight guy with a sweet body who would make for a terrific fling. Get it out of my system. That's what I would do.

Parker had fallen to his knees, one hand clutching the rail and the other clutching his stomach. "Go below," I said, feeling a stab of pity.

"You sure you can get us home?" he asked.

"It's a squall, Parker, not a hurricane. And look, there's the lighthouse." I pointed to the dull light in the distance.

"Thank the Lord." Parker gathered himself up and stumbled below decks.

It began to pour just as I berthed the *Queen*. I secured her and went down to check on Parker. I found him lying on the bed in the fetal position, clutching a pot to his chest.

"We are safely at harbor," I said.

"Then why are we still pitching?" he asked, looking up at me with sad green eyes.

"Because the boat is still in the water," I said, maybe a bit too sharply. Things were a lot calmer in the harbor; we were hardly pitching anymore.

Parker sat up and put down the pot which was, thankfully, still empty. "I don't know if I'm cut out for a life at sea," he said.

"Not much of fisherman, are you?" I said. I hadn't believed much about Parker's past, but I had believed the fishing part. I'd seen his hands, after all. His thumbs were callused in all the right places. And he'd applied for a job on a boat. It seemed to add up. Until now.

"I haven't been completely honest with you," he said.

"No kidding."

"Yeah. It's Murray who's the fisherman. Me, I worked on the docks. I was in fish canning."

"So you canned fish? In Canada? A Canadian fish canner." I didn't believe him. I think he knew I didn't believe him. But who was I to kick a guy when he's seasick? Besides, he was a quick study and if he could get past the up-chucking, he might actually make a decent assistant. And Pop liked him. And he could cook.

"It'll get easier, on the boat," I said. "And next time, we'll have clear sailing."

"Can I have that in writing?" he said.

"Nope," I said. "You'll just have to trust me."

166

Chapter Twenty Eight

Marco

Tell the truth, I hated those damned sharks with their flashy teeth and their poisonous barbs. Reminded me of Phil and company, the way they snapped snaggle-toothed, eyes empty as death. But mostly, I hated them because of the way Nik looked at them, like they were the most beautiful creatures in God's blue sea. I couldn't for the life of me see what she saw in those things, but there it was.

I wasn't so crazy about the sea. For a minute there, I had figured I could pull off the whole fishing thing. Course, Nik probably had me figured when I steered into the piling. But hell, I could have told her that it was a big boat and a pleasure cruiser to boot. It was like driving a Hummer if you were used to a Bug, I could have said. And I might have gotten away with it if the sea hadn't ratted me out. That sea has no mercy, the way it tossed the *Queen* around like she was a chew-toy. The way it turned me into a sniveling little kid afraid of the dark. When that first swell hit us, I tossed chow all over the deck.

Nik had laughed the storm off, a cosmic joke. Nothing more than a day's work. I'd been diminished. That's what got me. In my life before P-town, I'd been the man. I'd been the one with the moves. And here I was, laying on a bed staring at obscene wallpaper, clutching the stockpot like it was my blankie. Jesus, Mary, and Joe, I had made a fool of myself. I can't say I liked it much.

When she came down, I had to fess up that I wasn't a fisherman. I made up some other story about my maritime past. I'm pretty sure she didn't believe me. And I figured that she'd probably send me packing.

She didn't send me packing, though. She took the pot and bought me a ginger ale from the vending machine, saying that it would settle my stomach. We drove home in the driving rain and I was so glad to be off that cursed boat that I said we should stop at the store and I'd make a nice marsala.

"You sure you're up to cooking?" she asked. I liked the concern in her voice. To tell the truth, I was feeling better since getting off the boat.

"I'd like to make amends," I said.

By the time I was back in the Silvas' kitchen, slicing mushrooms with old Nick watching as though slice and stir was the best show in town, I was feeling like my old self again. I went so far as to boast about my knife, the one with the Swiss blade I'd been forced to leave behind.

"Forced, you say?" asked Nick, and Nikki, who had come into the kitchen four times already, also turned her dark eyes on me.

"Forgot to pack it," I said, "when I left."

I flipped the current, somewhat dull, knife in the air and started chopping the basil, hoping to distract father and daughter with the dazzle of my knife.

"So you learned to cook in Canada by watching the Food Channel?" Nikki raised her brows.

"Yeah, that's right. And I took this class at a place in Halifax, which was where we were living." It was a good thing I'd studied up on the Maritimes. "At this gourmet place. The guy teaching said that a good knife was the most important part of cooking. Course, he was trying to sell knives. But he had me, so I bought one."

"Right," said Nikki.

"Well, knife or no," said Nick, "you sure do got a knack."

Chapter Twenty Nine

Nikki

He was a smooth liar, I'll give him that much. For all I knew, he *had* learned to cook at a gourmet shop in Halifax. Though I would have bet good money that none of what he said was true. I didn't call him on it. I could have. Maybe I should have. But the fact was that Pop believed he was a research guy who had lived in Canada for a time. If Pop knew that Parker had found me through one of Jeremy's fliers and that he'd been homeless and that I didn't ask for references, that, in fact, Parker had no references, he would have thrown a fit and he would have thrown Parker out.

If I exposed Parker for the fraud he was, my father and brothers would never let me live it down. They would have gone and added impulsive to the list of my faults. And damned if they wouldn't have been right. For all I knew, Parker could have bodies in a freezer somewhere. But really? I knew the minute I met Parker that he wasn't a killer. He was way too scared for mass murder.

Over the past few weeks, I'd come to trust Parker Bench. Parker may have been one of the most honest people I'd ever met. I know that makes no sense at all. Call it gut instinct, call it intuition, call it whatever. Fact was, I trusted him despite himself. More than that, I liked him. Maybe a little more than I should have. He wasn't hard to look at and he was one hell of a cook. The marsala he made that night was, as Pop put it, "A little taste of heaven." Pop, mind you, is not given to poetic hyperbole.

We were feeling so contented after our good meal, in fact, that when Viddie came by to announce that Tripp's grand opening had been postponed by a week because of some flooding in the Shoppe's basement, we all managed to look sufficiently disappointed. We even promised, absolutely, that we would come. And when she wondered aloud whether or not to invite Father Eli to the festivities, Pop said that he was sure Eli loved a good beach toy as much as anyone.

We sent Viddie happily on her way and spent the rest of the evening inventorying Pop's stuff. Saturday would mark another opening, that of the Wellfleet Flea market and Pop, Parker, and I piled box after box in the garage next to the bedroom set.

Parker, it seemed, also had a knack for organizing. He labeled each box not only with the contents inside, but with a price that he and Pop had decided on. There were receipt checks and a cash box at the ready. There were two folding tables and a few lawn chairs setting up the store. We loaded what we could onto the back of my truck, then I called Ella to ask if we could borrow Harry's truck. I had to make the call, because Pop and Ella still weren't speaking.

Late Friday, Parker and I went over to Harry and Ella's to collect the truck. Ella invited us in for lemonade. "I owe you an apology," said Parker, as Ella handed him a glass.

"Why? You do something I don't know about?" asked Ella.

"I think me going to see Eli gave Nick the wrong idea about Billy."

Parker took a sip. "Anyway, I'm going to stop going. To see Eli."

"So you've finally seen the light. Hallelujah," I said. Parker gave me a pained look.

"If my going causes friction between your Pop and Billy, then it's not worth it."

"It's not worth it anyway," I said.

"You don't really think you can change, do you?" asked Ella.

"I thought I could maybe. I'm not sure," said Parker, shrugging.

At the break of dawn on Saturday, Pop and Parker loaded up Harry's truck. They made such a racket that any thought I'd had of sleeping in went out the window. Not that I wasn't glad that Pop and Parker were getting along. I just wondered that they got along as well as they did. Parker had been a stranger only a month before and Pop, if he was anything at all, was wary of strangers.

I helped them load the last of the stuff, then Parker asked if I wouldn't like to come along. I told them I had planned to go down to the *Queen* to get her ready for Monday's outing and to swab the decks. Parker went a little pale, and I wasn't sure if it was the swabbing or the thought of another day on the water that made him blanche.

"Come on, girl," said Pop. "Parker can help swab her down later. We could use the help."

Pop nodded to Parker, who swallowed visibly. "Sure. Right. Part of the job description, right? Swabbing?"

I figured that the more time Parker spent around chum and fish guts, the better he'd be able to stomach it. So I agreed to the compromise: flea market now, swabbing later.

"Great," Parker said, though it looked like he wasn't entirely convinced.

I hadn't been to the flea market since I was a teenager. My mother had a thing for tag sales and antiques, so she would go at least once during the season. When I was a kid, I'd usually go with her. We always came home with some trinket or another, a cuckoo-clock one year, a turtle-shaped soup tureen the next. Pop would complain that we didn't need to cram the house with junk, but Mama would just smile and pat his hand and say it was a bargain and a useful bargain at that. I guess it was kind of bittersweet that Pop had taken to cramming the house with his own useful bargains those past few years. Maybe it was a sort of quiet tribute to my mother's memory, though I never would have suggested this to him. If I had, he probably would have pointed out the vast difference between old junk and the brand new and very practical items he had amassed.

The fair-like atmosphere of the flea market, the smell of fried dough scenting the air, the dusty old knick-knacks lined on tables, the crafts and the glassware and the Tshirts and leather wallets brought those old memories back. They were happy memories and I was glad to be in the midst of all that bustle and even gladder that I could make myself useful in helping Pop to set up the table with his wares.

Pop had brought along three lawn chairs and the three of us sat in the sun, one of us jumping up to wait on the occasional customer. Most of the folks who stopped by were more interested in browsing than in buying and as the morning wore on it became clear that my services weren't really needed. So I got out pen and pad and began redesigning the population count to include a behavioral study of the sharks Parker and I had tagged. I got so involved in my ideas that I failed to notice Eli until his shadow darkened the page. I put down my pen.

"Work?" he asked. He was wearing jeans and a Holy Cross sweatshirt, looking so much like the boy I remembered that I tapped the schematic I'd been drawing, trying to get hold of myself.

"Yes," I said, and to further right the feelings crawling up and down my spine I began explaining population counts and behavioral patterns. I rambled on for a few minutes before Eli took the pen that I was still tapping.

"We need to talk," he said.

"I was talking," I said. "Maybe you weren't listening."

"You haven't changed. Still as contentious as ever."

I took the pen back. "I don't know that we have anything to say to each other." I began sketching a dogfish at the bottom of the page. Pop had just finished explaining the value of a button-holer to an unsuspecting browser and Parker had come back with a tray of coffees from a nearby vendor, Jeremy and Billy following in his wake.

"Well, well," said Jeremy, once he saw me. "If it isn't the little boat wrecker herself."

"Jer," Billy began in a warning tone, but Jeremy was on a roll, berating me for the chummy mess I'd left above decks.

"It was raining. Hard," I explained. "And my assistant had taken ill." All eyes turned to Parker, who looked like he was considering a hasty get away in the truck. Jeremy corralled him before he could make a break for it and put a proprietary arm around him.

"Sea sick? Oh, that is a terrible feeling," said Jeremy. "I wanted to die the first time out to sea. D. I. E." He shook Parker with each letter, causing the coffee he was carrying to slosh onto the tray.

"I was going to change his name to Hurl," I said. To which Parker and Jeremy both shot me a look. "It's a joke. Jeez." What was it with these guys? My brothers, at least, knew how to take a joke.

"So where were you last night?" asked

Billy, always the peacemaker.

"Home. Why?"

"You missed the big tadoodle," Billy glanced at our father, who grinned at the word 'tadoodle' despite himself.

"Good Vibrations. The grand opening." Jeremy took his arm from around Parker and executed a flourish.

"What's Good Vibrations?" Eli asked.

"Tripp's new store," Pop said. "Beach toys."

"I suppose you could use them on the beach," Jeremy said. "A little kinky, but why not?"

"I thought that was next Friday. Aunt Viddie said." I stopped myself. "Was Viddie there?"

"Big shock, she was not," Jeremy said.

"I can understand why, I guess," Billy said. To which Jeremy began a rendition of "Good Vibrations" while making an obscene gesture. Parker nearly dropped the coffee and Eli was trying hard to hide a smirk.

"Holy shit," I said, "with a marshmallow stuck in the middle."

"Such a quaint turn of phrase," Jeremy said.

"So let me get this straight," Pop said. "It's not a toy store?"

Billy couldn't even look at our father; his face had gone three shades of crimson.

"Oh, it's a toy store," I said, feeling as hot as Billy looked. Pop still looked confused and I thought I could explain it to him, but no, I was no better than Billy in this.

It was Eli who said, "They sell toys of a

different kind. Private toys."

"A sex shop?" asked Pop. "Viddie's boy is running a sex shop?"

"It looks that way," Billy said.

"Well, hot damn," said Pop. Then he started to laugh.

Chapter Thirty

Marco

Nick Silva thought his nephew's new business was about the funniest thing he'd heard all year. He went so far as to suggest that we all pay a little visit to old Tripp's Shoppe after Mass the next morning. He'd be sure to bring Viddie. "About time she was taken down a peg or two where that dumb-ass kid of hers is concerned," he said.

We unloaded about a quarter of our inventory that day and ended up putting the rest back on the truck. This did not faze Nick in the least, who blamed it on a downturn in the economy and the fact that tourist season wasn't in full swing yet. Nick, I got to say, seemed pretty happy to hang on to his stuff for another week. The stuff didn't worry me much, either. I was going to help Nick re-sell the bedroom on eBay and we'd already rented a table for the next week.

As for Tripp, I can't really say I cared a lot, but Nick wanted to talk about him. "She and Martin only had the one boy, understand. She always thought that kid hung the moon and swung around on it, despite the fact that the boy couldn't hang his own pants on a nail. Then she has the nerve to say what she did about Billy."

"His being gay, you mean?"

Nick shifted behind the box he was hauling to the truck. "I tell you, any one of my kids is worth two Tripps, including my Billy. And if you tell any of them that, I'll never talk to you again. That's the whole trouble with Tripp. Viddie filled him up with so much nonsense his head's so swelled that it's a surprise he can move hither and yon."

When Nick got going on something, he could talk your left ear off. I kind of hoped the talking jag would continue, because Eli and Nikki were sitting across from each other at a picnic table in front of the fried dough stand looking mighty cozy. Nick snorted when I pointed this out to him. "Those two," he shook his head. "If you'd of bet me back in the day, I'd have wagered they'd of been married by the week after they graduated high school. My wife kept saying they were too young and that our Nikki was too headstrong for a gentle kid like Eli. She turned out to be right on that one.She was right about a lot of things, was my Mary, God rest her."

"So they were a couple."

"Oh hell, from back in the eighth grade. Funny, how things turn out."

"What do you suppose they're talking about?" I said, wondering if it was about me and hoping that Eli would spill the beans and at the same time praying to God he wouldn't.

"Being as they went over there to talk in private, I don't suppose it's any of our business." Nick picked up another box and turned his attention toward loading the truck.

Chapter Thirty One

Nikki

Sitting across a picnic table from Eli with a large fry doused in ketchup between us felt about as natural as breathing. Back when we were kids, Eli would take my drink and, pushing the straw between his lips, would take a deep sip and pass the drink back to me. At seventeen, I thought this was about the sexiest thing that could happen between two people and maybe I wasn't so wrong about that. That was twenty years ago and now we were reduced to the politeness of near strangers: "Would you care for fries?" "No thank you." "How about a coke?" "Yes, a coke would be nice."

When we sat with the fries and drinks, an awkward silence settled across the table until, unable to stand the heaviness of it a minute more, I asked what he wanted.

"How are you?" he asked.

"How am I? I'm fine, Eli. I'm right as rain."

"So here we are. Both of us home again," he said.

"So here we are, both of us home again."

Eli glanced over to Pop and Parker,

loading the folding tables onto Harry's truck. "You and your dad seem very taken with Parker Bench," he said.

"And your point is?"

"I'm just...I just don't want you to get hurt."

"If you tell me that you still care about me, I'll dump the fries in your lap," I said.

"Look, there's been a lot of water under the bridge since...and you and I, we're both grownups now. But...I know you, Nikki. At least I used to. And I know that you have a tendency not to look before you leap."

"Is that what you figure happened, Eli? I leapt before looking?"

"This isn't about us. It's about Parker. About your family and...What do you know about him, really?"

"Parker Bench needed a little help and we're helping him. That's all."

"Really? That's all?"

"Despite all of your interventions, Father Avellar, Parker still prefers peckers to boobs, so I'd say your, whatever the hell it is, let's call it concern, is unfounded. So quit it." I didn't dump the fries. Though I did get up and walk away. The same way I'd walked away a long time ago.

After running Harry's truck back to his place, Parker and I got into my truck and headed for the pier. Parker had been sending me glances ever since my encounter with Eli, as though he were trying to observe me without my noticing. When I finally asked him about it on the way to the pier, he said. "Your truck is a mess. And it smells awful." He pulled a Dunkin Donuts bag from behind the seat and held a stale, half-eaten donut up as evidence. "You doing a little roach research later?"

"Shut up," I said. Though he probably had a point. I'd been transporting chum and seal carcass, and in light of that, a few stale crumbs didn't seem so daunting. I was miffed though, probably as much at Eli as at Parker. Probably because it was just like Eli to take the high road of concern for my family and probably because it was just like me to let him do it. It had always been like that. Me, the strong-willed girl with too much ambition and Eli, the good boy who would put me on the straight and narrow. No wonder we couldn't make it work.

I pulled into the Dunkin Donuts lot. Just past the drive-through was a garbage can. I took the bag from Parker and dumped it. "Anything else, Mr. Clean?" I was blocking the patrons behind us who, having paid for a new bag to mess up their own car, were in a hurry to get on with it. They beeped. "Well?"

Parker handed me an empty cup, a half-eaten bag of chips, and a container that had cream cheese in it. I threw them all into the trash. The driver behind me rolled down his window and gave me the finger.

"Are we done?" I asked.

Parker crossed his arms and stared at me. "I sincerely hope I've met your housekeeping standards," I said. Then I hit the gas. Finger man nearly back-ended me at the exit. Some people don't know the meaning of patience.

The rain had cleared the deck pretty well. It wasn't nearly as bad as Jeremy had made it out to be, which only added to my belief that he was the world's biggest fuss budget. "I cannot believe that my baby brother wants to marry that man," I said, taking the mop and bucket out.

"Maybe they won't get married."

"I thought you and Pop and the good Father had given up on trying to trade to the other team."

Much as I hated to admit it, Eli was right that we knew next to nothing about Parker Bench. In the mood I was in, I might have beaten the truth out of my assistant. I might have, if Max Groper hadn't come on board to ask me how I felt about whales.

Four humpbacks had beached at First Encounter on the tidal flat in Eastham. Since they were a little short-handed at Coastal Studies, he was wondering if I might lend my expertise. Of the four, one had been rescued and sent back to deeper water, two were hanging in, and the fourth had already died. "I can't pay you," Max said, "but I could offer up dead whale parts for compensation. Sharks would like that, I imagine."

"I've never tried whale before," I said, "but, given the fat content, I think the sharks would like it very much."

Chapter Thirty Two

Marco

Jesus and Joe, the woman was going to be the death of me. She was all excited about the whale business. It wasn't so bad at first. We spent all of Saturday and most of Sunday afternoon getting the two live whales back into the water and we managed to save them both. I'd never been that up close and personal with a marine mammal. They smelled God awful, like a whole fish store had lost refrigeration on a ninety degree day.

The worst smell was wafting off the dead whale, still on the side of the beach. Because of where he'd beached up or something, they couldn't haul him back into the water or get him out of there. The neighbors were complaining and who could blame them? Smell like that could affect the value of beach front property big time.

Monday morning, Nikki and I drove back down to First Encounter with a couple of chainsaws in the back of the truck. Nik was acting like it was Christmas Eve and I couldn't think of a worse job than butchering up a rotting dead whale. Butchering rotting dead whales was one of the jobs I figured they had in hell. I told Nikki as much.

"You survived the seal. The whale will be easy."

"We going to put the whole twenty tons on the truck or just the good parts?" I asked.

But even before we got to the dead whale, there was Sunday. After Mass and before we went down to help out the whales, Nick Silva had sidled up to his sister Viddie and said that it was a doggone shame that she'd gotten the date of the opening wrong.

Viddie told him that she hadn't gotten it wrong. There had been a flood in the basement and Tripp was trying his darndest to get the place up and running. It was something, she said, the way that he was taking responsibility. He was practically a hero, she said, getting that Shoppe ready for tourists. To which Nick suggested that they go have a look-see, maybe help the hero out.

"What are you trying to do, kill her?" Nikki asked when we got home on Sunday afternoon. Nick was waiting for us so that we could pick up Viddie and head down to the store.

"Just trying to get her to see what's what," said Nick. "The woman has lived in her own little world for too long."

Nikki's eyes were virtually dancing at the thought. "Good thing I'm coming along," she said. "I know CPR."

"Are you sure you want to do this?" I asked. To which two pairs of dark Silva eyes stared at me.

"We're sure," Nick said.

"We're very sure," Nikki said.

Good Vibrations was in an alley off Commercial Street, the main drag in Provincetown. From the outside the store could have been just about anything, a bakeshop maybe, or one of those places that sells hats and jewelry. Or an honest-to-God beach toy store for that matter. A purple and pink stripped awning shaded the shop's front window. In the window was the same purple and pink material draping a display case, a small hand-painted sign, and a few beach shells and such.

Viddie thought the display was enchanting. That was the very word she used after she put her nose up to the glass as though there were maybe fresh-baked pastries on the other side of the window. The inside was pretty tasteful, considering.

My first thought would have been jewelry store and there was actual jewelry on display, rings and bracelets and such, in the center case by the cash register. It took a good look around to figure out what Good Vibrations was all about. Even after I'd had my good look around, it seemed like Viddie was pretty oblivious. Though Nick, being confronted with the tangible evidence of what his nephew was peddling, mumbled something about needing a cool drink and beat a hasty retreat back to the alley.

The girl behind the counter, a blade-thin blonde who couldn't have been too far out of high school, walked over to the shelf where

Nikki had taken up a purple model and was examining it the way she had examined the tracking equipment we'd gotten for the *Queen*.

"It has a power switch." The girl showed Nik a tiny hidden button and pushed it. The thing began gyrating around like an overexcited snake. Nikki must have been thinking snake too because she asked, without cracking a smile, if the thing hissed. The girl, also without cracking a smile, said that in fact it didn't and pointed to a suggestion box set up on the counter.

"Gift?" asked the girl, "or private use?" She was eying the two of us, Nik and me, with the kind of serious like we were out to buy some new stemware or something. Nik, intrigued by the purple snake, was turning the thing off and on and on and off. And me, when the girl said private use, had such a vision in my head about me and Nik that I nearly left the store. And, of course, that vision like a film loop kept going around and around.

"Oh my." Viddie's voice broke into my little movie like a ringing phone. A wake- up call. "Oh my dear goodness."

"Interesting, isn't it?" Nikki switched the dildo on and handed it to her aunt, who didn't take the handoff, and so let the thing drop onto the floor where it danced around in a little circle.

"I'm afraid we've got the wrong place," Viddie said.

The girl, still as serious as a surgeon about to cut into a chest, said

"We don't have what you're looking for?"

"Beach toys." Viddie clutched the little starfish broach pinned to her blouse. "Looking for."

"There's a T-shirt shop just over on the main drag. I think they sell boogie boards and stuff," said the girl, trying to be helpful.

"Boogie boards," repeated Viddie, her face gone the same coral as the starfish. Enough was enough, I thought. I took the poor woman's arm and said that maybe she ought to sit down. To which the girl grabbed a stool from behind the counter. Together, we sat Viddie down.

Nikki picked up the vibrator, turned it off, and set it carefully back into the display stand. "Does it come with the stand?" she asked the girl.

"No," said the girl, "but it does come with a velvet carrying case. Batteries are extra."

"Oh my." Viddie might have fallen off the stool if I still hadn't had a hold of her arm.

Nikki patted her aunt on the shoulder and went to the display case, "What are those?" she asked, pointing down into the case.

"Nipple rings," said the girl. "The small ones can be used as labial rings. Do you have a piercing?"

"No, afraid I don't," Nikki said. Viddie's eyes took on the look of someone who was hypnotized. Only it wasn't all the talk about piercings. It was Tripp, newly come in from out the back of the store carrying a box.

"We're putting these in the..." he said, before catching sight of his mother and

189

dropping the box. A dozen dildos rolled around on the floor like frightened mice. Viddie fell off the stool. I quickly caught her arm as she started to tip, but I couldn't keep the stool from getting knocked over. The stool and Viddie both plowed into me and the two us fell to the floor in a kind of slow motion.

Tripp got down on his knees in front of us. "What are you doing here?" he asked.

"Checking out your new place of employment." Nikki picked up the scattered dildos and put them back in the box. She took hold of a black one that looked like it was made out of marble. "Nice," she said.

The girl had gotten a glass of water from the storage room. She handed it to Tripp, who gave it to his mother, who took a sip, then coughed and sputtered as though the water was going to drown her. She grabbed Tripp's arm. "This is your store?" she asked when the sputtering had stopped.

Tripp nodded.

"You sell?" Viddie asked.

"Toys," said Tripp quietly.

"And people buy these...toys?" asked his mother, still clutching Tripp's arm.

"Oh yes," said the sales girl. "This store is the fifth of its kind. We have stores in Manhattan, Key West, Los Angeles, Boston, and now here."

"It's a good business," said Viddie, as Tripp and I helped her back to her feet.

"It's a great business," said the girl. "We're putting out a web catalog in the fall. We'll be bigger than LL Bean someday."

"LL Bean," Viddie said.

"I'm Gayle, by the way," the girl said. "Gayle Priva. I'm the manager at this location."

"No, you're not," said Viddie. "Tripp said..."

"He's the other manager," I said, looking pointedly at the girl. Nikki snorted.

The girl, not catching my drift, said, "Actually..."

"We've got to get going," I said. "See where Nick's gone off to. Just wanted to stop by, say good luck and all that."

I took Viddie's arm and steered her to the door. Nik picked up the last of the dildos and handed the box to Tripp. "Great stuff," she said, before following us out.

"Well then," said Viddie, looking at the display window once we were outside. "Isn't that interesting? A lucrative business, that's what that Gayle said. Well, of course it's a lucrative business. Tripp is very innovative. He has a nose for business."

"Good old Tripp," said Nikki.

Chapter Thirty Three

Nikki

Aunt Viddie missed her calling, I think. She should have been in PR. This is what I told Parker as we headed down towards Eastham and the dead whale on Monday morning.

"You really want to see the old girl suffer?" he asked. He kept his eyes on the road. I think he was pretty sure he knew what I'd say to that.

Viddie had spent most of her life as judge and jury of her brother's family. Harry married too young. Pete married a non-Catholic, which of course ended in divorce. I was too smart for my own good. I left behind a nice boy and wasted a chance at a good marriage for some crazy schooling that made no sense, and no wonder my life was in the state it was in. Don't even get her started on Billy. Because Billy, of all things, chose to be gay.

"And Tripp works as a sales clerk in a dildo store," I said to Parker. "And she says, 'Well, isn't that nice? What a terrific business.'"

We made the turn by the windmill at the Eastham town green and started heading for the beach.

"Why are you so angry?" Parker asked.

"I'm not angry," I said.

"Yes, you are. So what if Viddie sees Tripp with a little bias? She's his mother. Somebody's got to stand up for him. So he's a dork. So what?"

"You don't know the half of it."

"You know what I think? I think you're angry at the whole world so they won't have to see how unhappy you are."

That cut it. I didn't want to be psychoanalyzed by some guy from God knows where running from God knows what. He'd known my family for what? A few weeks?

I pulled the truck over to the apron, got out, and slammed the door. I began walking down the road. I realized after about a hundred yards what a spectacularly stupid thing I'd done. I should have kicked Parker out of the truck. It was my truck, after all. Having set the wheel of fate in motion, I had no choice but to follow through. So I pulled my shoulders back, sucked in a deep breath, and kept right on walking. I heard the truck pull off the shoulder behind me, then Parker passed me by.

I trudged on towards the beach, while in my head calling Parker all manner of names, lambasting him for leaving me. Firing him from the job he didn't have, in fact. Over the hill, at the junction of the bike path, I saw the truck pulled over. Parker had gotten out and was standing with one foot on the running board staring pensively into the wind. He looked like he could be on the cover of a romance novel, but I was not about to be moved. I indulged in a short fantasy in which I pushed him aside, slammed the door in his face, and sped off, leaving him with the bike racks. Let him walk his way all the way back to P-town.

"Okay, I'm sorry," he said, as I drew closer. "I crossed a line and I'm sorry." He looked good standing there, the ends of his dark hair blowing around, his green eyes on me. My heart did a little turn. But I wasn't ready to let him off the hook just yet.

I climbed into the passenger side and without another word, Parker climbed into the driver's seat and shut the door. "Nikki," he began. I didn't want to hear sorry again.

"Last I heard there was still a dead whale on the beach," I said, "so move it."

There was nary a parking spot to be had at First Encounter. This was noteworthy because the parking lot is exceptionally large and a weekday morning in May is hardly prime time for beach goers. Add to this that the tide was out, which on the tidal flat meant you'd have to walk a mile to get to swimmable water.

"You think this is on account of the whales?" Parker asked, pulling the truck onto the sandy shoulder alongside the marsh.

"Duh," I said. Of course it was the whales. Although the whales had been reduced to whale and dead whale at that. I couldn't much see the point of bringing the kids out to gander at a dead whale.

"So we're going to chainsaw a whale in front of all these witnesses?" Parker asked.

I gave him the evil eye. "The chainsaw is a last resort," I said. Which was true, although being as most of the other avenues had been tried, I didn't see we had much choice but to butcher the whale and cart it away. In front of all these witnesses. Even so, I left the chainsaw in the truck bed. For now, anyway.

Parker and I made our way past the milling crowd, or gawking crowd to be more accurate, to the beach. The whale lay just inside the tide line. The boundaries around the carcass had been staked out and were festooned by crime tape as though the whale had been murdered by thugs and CSI would be sent in to investigate. As it was, I wouldn't have been surprised if a forensics unit had shown up. The place was crawling with every sort of official in the Commonwealth of Massachusetts. Parked on the beach were two State Police cars, several local police sedans, a host of fire trucks, and a van that said SWAT Team.

I saw Max Groper among the official crowd at the crime scene. "Can you believe this nonsense?" he said, flailing his arms like a sea gull trying to take flight in a stiff wind. "You'd think these bone heads would know better. You'd think they'd never seen a beached whale before. But no. Hell no. Don't take any advice from someone who might actually know something. Oh no, let the cops handle it."

"Quite the response team," I said. "Did

you dial 911?"

Max rolled his eyes. "Some woman called to complain about the smell. Made her beach walk less than pleasant, she said. I explained to them that it was a new moon and the tide just isn't coming up very far. A week would do the trick. We could tow it out to sea once the tide situation changes. Next week. But God forbid it sit there a week. Then I suggested that you and I cut the thing up and cart it away. But heavens, then we'd have whale parts on the beach and we can't have that, can we?"

As Max finished his tirade, I glanced at the whale carcass. It was a massive thing, stuck on a sandbar not a hundred yards from the main beach. The birds had begun doing cleanup, though it was an awful lot of carrion for a bird feast. And, with the wind coming off the bay, the smell was, to say the least, unpleasant. Several onlookers had pulled their jackets over their mouths and noses. Parker looked like he wanted to do the same.

"Should I get the chainsaw?" I asked.

Max looked at me as if he thought I hadn't heard a word he'd said. But they needed to dispose of the body and they wanted to do it today, so I didn't see we had much choice.

"You aren't going to be allowed to butcher the whale in front of the crowd."

"So send the crowd away," I said.

"Oh, no. Oh, no. These geniuses have got a better idea. They're putting dynamite under the carcass as we speak."

"What?" Now it was me who questioned

my ability to hear.

Max nodded like a bobble head. "That's right. Dynamite. Just try to talk them out of it. We have half a dozen ocean people here, but oh no, they've got it figured out."

"Kind of gives a whole new meaning to 'there she blows,' huh?" Parker said. To which Max gave him an icy stare.

"Not funny," Max said.

"Actually, it kind of was," I said, to which Max turned the icy stare on me. Having grown up with three brothers, I was immune to the death-ray stare, so I ignored it and made my way past a local cop doing crowd control.

"Sorry, folks," the cop said. "This is as close as you can get."

"I'm Max Groper," said Max with an indignance that grew when the Statie didn't recognize the name. "Max Groper. From Coastal Studies? "

The cop stared blankly at Max. "Dr. Silva," I said, holding out my hand. "Massachusetts Bay Commission." I wasn't part of the commission strictly speaking, but with Ned's incessant need for publicity, who'd quibble when there was a dead whale body stinking up the beach? The cop brightened as soon as I said the magic words.

"The fish folks?" he asked.

"That's right. These are my colleagues."

"Oh." The cop glanced around as though trying to decide what to do with us. "I think we've got the whale situation covered."

At that point, a guy in a jacket labeled SWAT came over. Our new cop friend introduced us.

"Oh, good," said the SWAT man, a guy named Herman LeBlanc. "Just the experts we need." Then he asked, with all due seriousness, how much TNT did we, in our expert opinions, think was necessary to blow up a whale carcass. "We've got ten tons under her," he said, "but we're thinking we ought to put down another ten. We want to make sure we get her good, in small enough pieces so the tide can take her out. If we can manage it."

Max looked like he was going to have an apoplexy. He put his hands to his head and called the whole idea fucking imbecilic.

I, on the other hand, realized that we could call them imbecilic all we wanted. Somebody wanted to blow up a whale and, come hell or high tide, they were going to blow up a whale. Besides which, I do have a little bit of bad girl in me. "Ten more ought to do her," I told Officer LeBlanc.

Chapter Thirty Four

Marco

In my lifetime I have learned, among other things, not to overcook veal and never to forget a woman's name the morning after. On that day I added another little ditty to my list: never blow up a dead whale with dynamite.

Max Groper had figured it for a horror show and so had washed his hands of the whole mess and stormed off to his van. Nikki, too, must have figured what would happen, but that woman likes trouble, I swear to God.

"We'd better stand back," she said, with the same amused mischief in her eyes that she'd had at Good Vibrations. The cops had, in fact, already pushed the entire crowd back, so Nik and I went to stand in the front line, so to speak, right where the lot meets the beach in front of the first row of cars.

"I wish I'd brought the video camera," Nik said. "I hope someone is recording this for posterity." I looked around and noticed at least three video cams trained on the whale, which was now being wired for a trip to kingdom come. "YouTube bonanza," said Nikki. "I'm surprised that the folks from Channel Four aren't here."

"Maybe we should go wait in the truck,"

I said. I had this bad feeling that flying whale parts wasn't going to be like the fountain light show at the Bellagio in Vegas.

"What, and miss the fun?" Nikki grabbed my arm so I couldn't make a run for it.

The explosion was spectacular, I'll give you that much. There were a lot of "Oh wows!" from the crowd. Which, about a half a second later became "Oh, my Gods." Because the chunks of whale that had flown high up into the air were now coming back down. And they were headed straight for the crowd.

Nikki decided that running for it might be an option after all. We headed towards Max's van, parked just two cars over. All around us, screaming people made for cars. Some of them, I heard tell later, took refuge in the two port-a-potties at the edge of the lot. The back doors of Max's van were unlocked and we dove in behind a speechless Max in the driver's seat just as whale pieces started to hit the pavement.

"It's fucking Armageddon," Max said, as Nikki sang, "it's raining whale."

"You don't have to be so all fired happy about it," Max said. "It's fucking undignified."

"That it is," Nikki said. "Totally and wholly and undeniably fucking undignified."

"Oh, shit," Max said. I would have thought this was just another comment about whale falling from the sky when I saw what he was looking at: a big piece of whale. Falling from the sky. And headed like a cruise missile straight for the van. "Incoming!" yelled Max, as he ducked under the steering column.

I pushed Nikki to the floor in the back of the van and threw myself on top of her. Maybe in my eulogy, she would reminisce about how I put myself between her and deadly whale parts. My heart raced and this position, lying there on top of Nik close enough to smell the salt on her skin, caused another reaction of which I am less than proud. I was pretty sure Nik could feel the reaction prodding her lower back. I was pretty sure that this would alter what she would say at my funeral.

The van shuddered as the whale hit the hood with a thunk. Max's head peeked out from under the steering column like a gopher poking out of a hole. "Holy crap," he said, which pretty much summed up the situation. There on the hood of the van was a part of the whale's head. The eye, still right there in the side of the head, stared through the windshield at us. We stared back and I was pretty sure that, in that twilight zone moment, my heroism and my embarrassment would be forgotten and forgiven.

Chapter Thirty Five

Nikki

First Encounter Beach looked like a scene out of a B-grade horror movie. Pieces of whale, large and small, lay splattered on the asphalt. Several cars had dented roofs and hoods. A large chunk lay in the crater it had made in the top of a port-a-potty where six onlookers had taken refuge. One recycling can was entirely crushed. By the grace of God, no one was hurt, though all the folks who had joined us to witness the exploding whale ambled around like extras in *Night of the Living Dead.*

Even the officials who had first devised this brilliant plan looked shell-shocked. Sergeant LeBlanc stood on the beach, staring mutely at the spot where the whale had recently been, a bullhorn hanging from one hand like a useless appendage. Max, Parker, and I picked our way through the carnage to his side. "I had no idea," said the Sergeant softly.

"No idea?" asked Max. "If you had spent a minute thinking instead of doing, you probably could have figured it out. What did you expect would happen, that the damned whale would vaporize?"

The sergeant, still looking to the tide line, shook his head. "No idea."

I took hold of the bullhorn. Gently, as so not to upset him further. "May I?" The sergeant didn't answer, which I took to mean yes. I raised the bullhorn. "If you could all please get in your cars and clear the area, we could begin cleanup," I said.

The people, no doubt all too glad to have some direction in the aftermath of such trauma, complied without complaint. The few cars that had taken a direct hit were towed away, and the cops were good enough to remove any remaining debris from the vehicles, and to offer up insurance numbers that could be called. Which made me wonder: Did State Farm cover whale damage? I thought now was not the time to ask.

Once everyone had been cleared, I brought my truck around and told the authorities that I'd take as many whale bits as the bed could hold. They were happy to help me load and, in this way, the whole disaster did have a silver lining in that we hadn't had to butcher anything. By the time the bed was fully loaded, the cops and Parker and even Max had overcome their shock and, in the way people often do in such events, had become a little punchy. They began tossing bits of blubber like footballs, going out for long passes on the beach. This went on for some time, then one of them, a rookie cop named Mike Stookie, discovered a missed piece lying in the dune grass.

"Holy shit," Mike said. "Is this what I think it is?" He brought the trophy to the group for inspection and apparently it was exactly what he thought it was. Which confirmed that the whale had indeed been a male.

A whale's penis is, as might well be imagined, whale sized. The guys passed the appendage around in a sort of awed silence. "What are we going to do with it?" Mike asked.

It was soon decided that whatever we did with it, it could not be taken to the tide line to be taken out by the sea with whatever else hadn't fit in the truck bed. To a one, the men in the group agreed that leaving the penis, well-preserved as it was, to be eaten by the fishes was a sacrilege of sorts. Even Max agreed with the sentiment.

"Maybe we could have it stuffed," Parker suggested. I must have looked at him slightly askance because he seemed to want to pull his head into his jacket. I was thinking of the moment when Parker had, with some sort of misguided chivalry, tackled me in Max's van and I'd felt, shall we say, a bit of his own anatomy prodding my back. It felt kind of empowering that I could get that kind of reaction from a guy like Parker, though I was sure it had embarrassed him considerably. I wasn't going to bring it up, Then, in a way, this whole whale penis business brought it up for me.

"Good Vibrations might be interested," I said, which made Parker blush in a very satisfying way. "It's bigger than any vibrator I've ever seen. Bigger than the blue angel. Or even the demon, for that matter." I smiled benignly as the men cleared their throats and the two other women present smirked.

"Stuffing it is a good idea," said Max. "We could put it on exhibit, maybe at the Natural History Museum in Brewster. Or at the Institute."

"Why not just have it bronzed?" I suggested. Again, I was purposefully ignored as the men began to decide on a taxidermist who could handle such a delicate matter.

One of the local cops suggested Nate Atkins. He did a lot of game fish, the cop said, and so he might be just the fellow for the job.

"You know Nate, don't you?" Max asked, and attention finally turned my way.

I did know Nate Atkins. He'd graduated from P-town High a few years ahead of me. He was known about town as a guy who loved road kill. Nate, it was rumored, stuffed every run-over animal he found on Route 6 between Orleans and P-town. He kept these trophies on the glassed-in front porch of his house for all to admire. Nate had never married, which was small wonder given the road-kill obsession. But, despite Nate Atkins' obvious creepiness factor, he was a good taxidermist. And so it was that Sergeant LeBlanc called him and I was enlisted to transport the appendage to him for preservation.

The boys laid the penis carefully atop the other cargo in my already over-laden truck bed and Parker and I made out way back to P-town. Carefully, of course.

My thought had been to put the whale on board the *Queen* and since there was still about half an hour of daylight left when we arrived at MacMillan Pier, Parker and I set to doing just that. We had just finished stacking the whale pieces, putting the penis aside so that it would not be used as shark bait, when Jeremy and Billy stopped by.

"What, pray tell," said Jeremy, wrinkling his nose, "is that?"

"That," I said, "would be whale."

"Oh, no. Oh no, no, no. You cannot have dead whale on the deck of my ship. Not now."

"You said I could use the *Queen* for research. This is part of my research. You said your boat is my boat."

"Of course you can use the boat. But the chef is coming tomorrow."

"He's coming back? Why?" I asked as Parker mimed stirring, eating, and gagging behind Jeremy's back while Billy tried hard not to grin at him.

"FYI, he is the star of our new venture. As it is, we need to wait until at least mid-July to open. Everything has gone wrong. The contractor wants money now. And so, I have come up with a plan," Jeremy said. "There just so happens to be a group of venture capitalists in Tokyo who think a landmark restaurant in a wonderful tourist destination such as ours is just the thing." I raised my eyebrows.

"The gay Japanese business alliance," Billy said. "They arrive on Friday."

"And the chef?" I asked.

"And the chef is doing what he does best," Jeremy said. "The chef is going to prepare a meal for our Japanese friends that will knock their topknots off."

"The chef is going to cook?" I said, "Where, in the galley?"

"No, silly," Jeremy said. "The galley's too small."

"We were hoping the Red Tomato's kitchen would be up and running," said Billy, "but the contractor says it will be another two weeks at least."

"So my darling has come up with a brilliant solution to our dilemma," said Jeremy, taking Billy's arm.

"It's nothing. I asked Ella if we could use the kitchen at the café. It's a commercial kitchen, a little small, but since Ella's only open for breakfast and lunch..."

"And Ella agreed."

"Well, yeah."

I sensed the hesitation in my baby brother's voice. "But?"

"But, well Harry and Pete had to get in on the act."

"What do you have to do?" I asked.

"A week on the *Two Sons*, high season," Billy mumbled.

"With pay?"

"Yes. Minus a fee for use of the kitchen."

"Slave labor for one week; you drive a hard bargain."

"Do not pick on my sweet boy," said Jeremy. "I have already shown him my undying gratitude."

I did not want to get into a discussion

about Jeremy's undying gratitude and neither, it seemed, did Billy. He wandered starboard, feigning interest in harbor activity. Which is how he discovered the penis, which we had tucked alongside the pilot house, out of plain sight. "Is that what I think it is?" Billy asked.

"I think it is," I said.

Jeremy went over to investigate and nearly fainted with glee at the discovery.

"It's going to be stuffed. Some guy named Atkins?" said Parker.

Chapter Thirty Six

Marco

If only Billy could see past Jeremy's good looks and charm, he'd get a load of how he was being played. Billy deserved better. It hit me that saying that kind of thing out loud would make me sound gay. Which was good, because I was supposed to be gay. And bad, because in my heart of hearts I hoped that Nikki, who didn't believe much of my story, would quit believing that part of it.

I had apologized for what happened in Max's truck on the way home. Tried to apologize anyway. I bungled it something awful, tongue-tied as a kid with a crush, I called it 'the incident'. After all that had happened on the beach that afternoon, Nikki honestly didn't have a clue what I was talking about. She looked at me with those big brown eyes of hers and said, "Which one?"

I felt myself go two shades of tomato. "Tackling you," I said into the hand I was coughing into. After that there was a long and very unfortunate silence in the cab.

Until finally, she said, "Forget about it." So both of us dropped the subject.

But here's the thing, the more Nikki believed the stuff about me being gay, the more I seemed to fall right into the gay guy role. Here we were, on the deck of a big purple boat with two gay guys, one of whom was this great guy I really liked and the other one who I just as soon throw overboard, discussing a whale penis. Not exactly the kind of tender moment a guy hopes for.

"Amusing as this is," Jeremy said, "you'll have to clear the carcass out of here."

"Let me use the boat tomorrow," Nikki said. "I promise that it will be all gone by the time the chef gets here."

"I suppose," Jeremy said.

And that's how it was decided that the whale, penis included, would stay on board until morning, when we'd bring the penis over to the taxidermy guy then go feed the dogfishes a nice stew of whale chow. After which we'd come back and swab up the decks so they'd be shipshape for the chef and the gay Japanese business alliance, who would be wined and dined on board come Friday.

"I didn't blow up the whale," Nikki said. We were sitting in a booth at Ella's Place, me and Harry on one side, Pete and Nikki on the other. Ella was making us breakfast before we ventured off to the taxidermy and out to sea.

"Blow the pecker off a whale, that's a record even for you." Harry held out his cup to Ella for a refill.

"At least I'm not taking advantage of our baby brother," Nikki said.

"Nobody's taking advantage. Billy offered to help. It was a fair exchange," said

Pete.

"Fair exchange, my left butt cheek." Ella frowned at Pete. "The two of you used me to get free labor."

"If anybody's doing any using around here, it's Jeremy Fine," Harry said.

"I think he's got a thing for the chef," said Nikki. "He gets all twittery talking about him."

"Jeremy twittery? No!" Pete said.

"You don't seriously think that Jeremy's cheating on Billy, do you?" asked Harry. Three pairs of dark Silva eyes turned to me. Like I was some kind of expert or something.

"I think Parker ought to make a play for Billy," said Nikki.

"Parker and Bill, I can see that," said Pete. "Do you like him?" he asked me.

I didn't know what to say, so I shrugged and said "Sure."

"He means, you know, like like." Harry rolled his cup through his fingers, a little smile in the corners of his mouth.

"Billy's a good looking guy," said Nikki, the little dimple in her cheek growing. "And you're hot stuff. You even cook better than Chef Boyardee."

"Leave the poor guy be." Ella put a hand on Harry's shoulder and refilled my cup. "I'm cutting you three jokers off," she said, pointing the pot at the Silvas. "Don't let them gang up on you."

"We weren't ganging up on him," Harry said. "You're the one who said Billy ought to think twice before marrying Jeremy."

"A lot of us should have thought twice,"

Ella said, "before waltzing down to the altar." We all watched as she sauntered towards the counter.

"You better get some flowers before you head home," Pete said.

"Maybe a nice diamond necklace, too," Nikki said.

"And Zales isn't going to cut it," Pete said. "Is the Hope Diamond available?"

"You guys should take your act on the road," Harry said. "Nik could blow things up while you told jokes, Petey."

With that, Harry got out of the booth, swaggered over to Ella, took her in his arms, and gave her a Hollywood-worthy smooch. "Catch you later, baby," he said to his wife.

"You best bring flowers," said Ella, smiling.

Chapter Thirty Seven

Nikki

Nate Atkins never did get the commission, which he later stated would have been the greatest in his life. For better or worse, the penis was not preserved for posterity. When Parker and I went to pick up the appendage, it was gone. In its place stood a sheepish looking Jeremy.

"Where's my penis?" I said, realizing the minute the words were out of my mouth just how dumb that sounded.

"Have you lost it?" said Jeremy, in a weak attempt at levity. I gave him a look conveying an unspoken 'don't mess with me.' I hadn't been sure that the look would work on someone as self-absorbed as Jeremy, but it did. He looked like he wanted to jump overboard. Had he attempted it, I would have let him. "Funny story," he said.

It was at this point that the chef, as per-usual dressed in his Zorro cape, came up from below decks. "Ah, Signora Silva," he said, in a fake accent that was somewhere between French and Italian with a few Dutch highlights thrown in. "And what was your name again?" he asked, closing in on Parker, who spit out "Parker" as though he would have liked to cudgel Chef Verdi on the head with it. "I must thank you, signora, for the most unusual and gracious gift," said the chef.

"Gift," I shot another bullet look at Jeremy who did a very satisfying cringe.

"Whale penis," said the chef with a chuckle. "Very amusing. The Japanese adore that sort of thing."

Jeremy's head began bobbing like a buoy in a storm. "Yes. They love the unusual, the Japanese."

"It's a delicacy in Japan."

"Yes. A delicacy."

"Wait a minute," said Parker, who suddenly looked a lot like he had that first day out to sea. "You plan on cooking it?"

"It is already, shall we say, pickling. I make a brine of vinegar and fine herbs."

I was at a momentary loss for words. No matter how ridiculous I'd thought the whole taxidermy adventure, pickling trumped it absolutely. I let go a small snort.

"It is amusing, is it not?" said the chef. "Very whimsical."

"It's rotted whale meat," I said.

"Nonsense. I sniffed him. He smelled fresh. He will be the center of tomorrow's feast. The crowning glory," said the chef.

"Well, okey dokey, then," I said, raising my eyebrows at Parker. "We still need the boat and the rest of the whale meat. Unless, of course, you wish to make a consommé."

There was to be no consommé, the chef assured us. And no boat. Jeremy took me by the elbow and explained that the boat would need to be prepared for the gay Japanese venture capitalists, who were, even as we spoke, gathering at the Tokyo airport with their Louis Vuitton suitcases for the long trip into the sunrise. At Logan in Boston, they would be met by five Lincoln Town Cars and whisked to the Provincetown Inn so they could refresh themselves for a sight-seeing tour and an evening meal to be served as the sun set over Provincetown harbor.

The *Queen*, belonging as she did to one of P-town's premier divas, would be decked out in twinkling lights, tables set in crisp sailor blue and white cloths, and sprays of roses. Which, Jeremy hoped, would cover up the stink of rotting whale blubber.

The whale parts would, of course, need to be carted away before the capitalists' eminent arrival.

"What am I supposed to do with a truck load of whale meat?" I asked Jeremy.

"It has to go. I don't know where." It was at this point that I wished someone would put a load of TNT under Jeremy.

"I don't like you," I said. "I never liked you. And I take back my blessing."

"As if we ever had your blessing, girlfriend. That whole family of yours is homophobic."

"Really? I like Parker. And I love Billy. It's you I can't stand and sexual orientation has nothing to do with it."

"You have an hour before the florist comes to measure the boat for swags."

"Fine. Is the new freezer working?"

"My new freezer? At the Tomato? Woman, you can't be serious."

"New freezer or use the whale as part of

the table arrangements. Your choice," I said.

"I don't like you, either," said Jeremy, handing me the keys to the Red Tomato.

"You can't marry that man," I said to Billy as we boarded the *Queen* later that afternoon. He had helped me haul the whale meat over to the Tomato's freezer and swab the decks. The freezer had been, as predicted, in fine working order. It was, in fact, the only thing working at Land's End thus far. Rich Langley of Rich's Beautiful Bouquets had finished measuring the deck and had gone back to his shop.

"I know." Billy opened two of the white folding chairs that had been stacked along the pilot house. He plopped down into one and I sat in the other.

"Why?" I asked.

"Why? You're the one who brought it up. Why do you think I can't marry him?"

"Because he is an arrogant S.O.B. and he's self-absorbed and he's a diva. The diva part I could get past, but you deserve better."

"I think he might be cheating on me," said Billy. "With Chef Penis."

"That makes him an arrogant, cheating S.O.B." I said. "Not to mention..." But I didn't finish it. Billy had his head in his hands. "Are you sure he's cheating?"

"No. Maybe. He's just spending so much time with that weasel. And the way he looks at him."

"Because if he is, I'll have him murdered. I'll kill him myself if the whale

216

doesn't finish him off."

"That's sweet of you, Nik," said Billy. "But I'm not sure. I'm not sure of anything right now."

"Harry and Pete will use him for fish bait," I said.

"I don't want him used for fish bait," said Billy. "That's the problem."

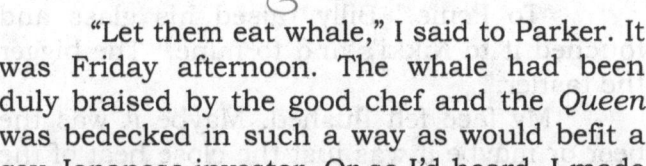

"Let them eat whale," I said to Parker. It was Friday afternoon. The whale had been duly braised by the good chef and the *Queen* was bedecked in such a way as would befit a gay Japanese investor. Or so I'd heard. I made it a point to stay away from the *Queen*.

Parker and I were at that moment seated at the bar of the Yard, a fishermen's hangout that neither gay Japanese nor divas would think to frequent. I'd asked Parker to come join Billy and myself for an evening of beer and darts. My little brother was sorely in need of someone who treated him well and I was not above playing matchmaker. I was pretty sure that both Parker and Billy saw through my ruse as I raised my glass. I was also pretty sure that there was hope for the two of them. Parker had all but said he thought Billy was attractive. Actually, he'd said that my brothers and I looked alike and that we were an attractive bunch after I pressed him about Billy. But who's quibbling?

Chapter Thirty Eight

Marco

"To Penis." Billy raised his glass and touched it to Nikki's and to mine. "The bigger the tastier."

My face felt flushed. Maybe it was the beer or maybe it was just the close heat of the dark bar. Or maybe it was that Nik was so obvious in playing matchmaker. Or that Billy didn't seem to mind that she was trying to fix the two of us up. To be honest, at that moment it had occurred to me that Billy's profile was a whole lot like his' sister's. I had thought about what it was a man would see in another man, curious, you understand. And I had thought that whatever that thing was, Billy had it in spades. Though not enough of it for me to be attracted. I was pretty good at pretending, I guess. But the truth was I could no more be gay than Billy could be straight.

That thought kind of got to me while I was sitting there nursing my beer. I had a bad case of the "if onlys." As in if only I hadn't told everyone in the Silva clan I was gay. If only I'd just played it straight, so to speak, I might be sitting on a deck with Nikki at some nice joint down on Commercial, at one of those tables with candlelight and we'd be looking into each other's eyes. Who was I kidding? Even if I had played it straight, Nik wasn't the kind of woman who would gaze intently into your eyes and declare her undying love. Nik would just as soon bite you.

Or so I thought until the door to the bar room opened and there, walking in the light that shone on him in as though he was walking in his own spotlight, was the mighty Thor.

Ned Anderson looked as out of place in that bar as Jeremy Fine would have. For one thing, he was the only guy in a suit. But he stood in that sliver of sun like he belonged right there among the beer drinking T-shirted fishermen. He looked around, found us at the bar, and strolled over with his hands down at his side like a gunslinger ready at any moment to shoot a hole in the mirror above the bar.

Nikki froze when she saw him. Then, catching herself, she took a pull of her raised glass and set it on the bar. Thor was a born politician. He smiled and shook hands with me and Bill, asked Bill how the restaurant was coming along but didn't really wait for an answer. He turned his baby blues on Nik and asked if he could have a second.

"Sure." Nik's hand, still on the beer, gave a little twitch. Only thing to betray her cool. "Grab a seat."

"Alone?" said Thor. It wasn't a question. More like the answer to a quiz that had been given that morning. And Nik, instead of being her usual stubborn self, got off the barstool and told me and Bill not to drink her beer.

"I hate that guy," said Billy, once the door had shut and left us in the dark taproom.

"Thor?" I said.

"Thor. I like that."

"He is kind of big and Nordic, isn't he?"

"He's a fucking Icelandic saga." Billy raised his glass. "To the mighty Thor and his mighty sword." After which he ordered another beer for each of us.

"Should we get one for Nik?" I said.

"She won't be back." And damn, ten minutes later when we'd each polished off a second glass, she was still AWOL. "Told you," Bill said. "To Thor the wonder Viking," he raised his glass and drained the remaining suds. "Her taste in men is worse than mine."

This was a shave too close for comfort. I wasn't sure I wanted to talk about Thor or what the two of them might or might not be doing.

"Should we stop them? Jeremy and the chef, I mean?" I said, after we'd polished off a third beer with still no sign of Nikki, and paid the tab, and made our way to the door.

We then made our way over to Ella's. No sign of Jeremy or the chef, but the smell coming out the kitchen wasn't a good ad for experimental cuisine and I got to thinking that Harry and Pete and Billy were all going to have to bring Ella roses for the use of her place.

"We should get over to the boat," I said.

"What's the big hurry?" said Billy, a little smirk painting the corner of his mouth. And there was that little bit of Nik again.

"He might get sued. You might get

sued. You're part owner of Land's End, right?"

"Very part," said Billy. "Miniscule part."

"How miniscule we talking?"

"Five grand. It was what I had left after... Let's just say I've made a few mistakes where business is concerned."

That much I knew. Nikki and the other Silvas had already told me about Billy's failed businesses. They were as much a part of family lore as was Nikki's blowing up the marina. "Chooses businesses like he chooses men," is what Nikki had said. She wasn't so wrong, given the way things were going for Billy. But who was I judge? Jesus and Mary, nobody was going to give me a prize for my life, either.

We took our time strolling from Ella's, up on the far end of Bradford, down to the pier in the center of town. Even from the parking lot you could pick out the *Queen*, all lit up like a big purple Christmas tree. Closer we could hear the *Queen*, too. A chorus of twenty gay Japanese venture capitalists, all losing experimental cuisine into the dark waters of the P-town Harbor.

"That whale penis certainly was amusing," said Billy, as he dialed 911.

Chapter Thirty Nine

Nikki

By the time I arrived on the scene with Ned, the ambulances were already dockside and the EMTs were already busy triaging casualties, sending the worst cases to Mid-Cape hospital in Hyannis for further treatment. Luckily, none of the revelers were gravely ill. Maybe I should have been more explicit in warning Jeremy. But any fool should know that using half-rotted whale meat as an entrée, no matter how amusing a whale penis might be, would only lead to disaster.

Billy called me right after he called 911. I can't say that I was happy to get the call. Though it had kept me from doing something nearly as stupid as eating whale penis. As I've said before, there is something about Ned that moves me to do stupid things. It's been that way ever since we met and, despite the fact that I am no longer in love with the man, that I, in fact, don't like the man very much anymore, it remained so even as he walked into the Yard the night of the great whale poisoning.

I'd caught Billy's look when Ned had sauntered up to my barstool, that 'oh no, not again' look he gets sometimes. I'd also gotten a load of Ned in an Armani suit, a suit that didn't suit him in the least. And damned if I didn't think he looked out of place. And that he'd look far better with the suit off.

Not that I had any plans for undressing him or myself. No. I was, in fact, ready to give Ned a dressing down for stonewalling on the grant. I was ready to stick it to him. Seems he stuck it to me instead. Sadly, without my even realizing it.

Without my realizing it, Ned had taken my hand and we were strolling down Commercial Street like the couple we used to be. Ned said it was a beautiful night and it was, too, one of those balmy spring nights that whispers of summer. On upper Bradford, the crowd thinned to a few tourists making their way to the guest houses scattered along the side streets. Ned and I kept walking, out past the Dairy Queen, talking about nothing in particular. Until a Land Rover drove too close to the road's shoulder spitting sand at our feet. Ned seized my arm and pulled me to the grass. "Wouldn't want to lose you," he said. And something in the way he said it brought me back to reality.

"What gives?" I asked.

"What?" said Ned, "I can't pull my beautiful ex-wife out of harm's way?" He let go my shoulders.

"You didn't drive up from Boston so that you and I could promenade under the stars."

Ned put his arm around me and pulled me in. "God, that's what I love best about you,

Nikki. You don't beat around the bush. Romance is lost on you."

I pulled away from him. "Didn't realize you'd come a courtin', Dr. Anderson. Might be a little late for us to spoon under the June moon. Being as you're practically re-married and all."

Ned sighed in that way he has, to let me know how totally impossible I was. "Can't we just be friends?"

"What, friends with benefits? I don't think so."

"I still care about you. I know you don't believe that. But it's true. It's why I drove all the way down here to give you the news."

"The grant came through?" I said, clutching his arm, more excited than I ought to be.

"Not quite."

I let go the arm. "Not quite?"

"It's a slow process, you know. Senator McGowan had asked for extra funding, but they're really cutting back in Washington. Nobody wants to be accused of ear-marking pet projects and well, there is no extra money. So I've had to cut a few things. And the grant, well..."

"Bottom line is there's no money for the study."

Ned shook his head sadly. "I can keep you on stipend. Maybe next year."

"Next year? I can't wait that long. I can't stay in limbo that long."

"I know, Nikki. I know." Ned stopped and pulled me into his arms. I could smell the soap he used, feel the soft fabric of the suit against my cheek. "Just hang in there, sweetheart. Hang in there and I'll do the best I can. I promise you." He leaned down and kissed me, gently, and damned if it didn't give me the shivers. "Please, just hang in," he said, as my cell phone rang.

It did not occur to me until later that I'd been played by Ned Anderson yet again. He'd said he had cut the grant. Which meant that he'd been the one to make the decision. Yup, I'd been played like a fine-tuned violin.

In my defense it would have occurred to me earlier if the wharf hadn't looked like a scene out of a disaster movie. The only one of the revelers not barfing into the harbor was Jeremy, who had (to his credit I suppose) thought better of eating the Chef's exotic victuals once he'd seen and smelled the entrée. Jeremy was instead pacing along the *Queen's* deck in an imitation of Captain Ahab in his less lucid moments. He had his hand over his mouth as though he, too, might bring up something bilious. Billy, with an empathy that was both enviable and infuriating, sat Jeremy down with an Oxycontin and a glass of ginger ale.

It wasn't until after the last of the ambulances had flashed away blue-lighted down Commercial Street, Billy had tucked Jeremy into the stateroom bed, and Ned had shaken his head and made a snide remark about how disaster seemed to follow me around like a stray puppy before bidding us farewell, that I plopped into the chair Jeremy had vacated on the ravaged deck and realized that Ned had done it again.

"Damn it all," I said aloud.

Parker, the only person still above deck, agreed. "Looks like hell, huh?" he said, pulling up a chair and sitting next to me.

"Quite the mess." I told Parker that no grant money would be forthcoming and that, since I didn't have a job, he didn't have one either. "Until such time as Senator McGowan can convince the good people on the hill that Stellwagen Bank isn't a barrel of pork."

"So you're firing me?"

"I can't fire you. I never hired you in the first place."

"So how good do you figure the senator will be at convincing the fools on the hill?"

"I wouldn't bet the boat on it."

"So we're out of work."

"Looks that way. I think the last bus back to my career has left the station. And I'm not on it."

"What bus we talking about?" asked Billy, coming up from below decks. "Good God, what a mess." He grabbed a third chair and sat beside us, the three of us all in a row looking towards the dark bay.

"How's Jeremy?" asked Parker.

"Blissfully asleep. He had a long day."

"Sleeping while Rome burns. Typical." I said.

"Rome's in ashes, sis."

"Jeremy's an idiot," I said.

"Yeah, but he's my idiot."

"You are not going back to him," I said, putting a finger to Billy's chest.

"He needs me."

"He cheated on you."

"I don't think he cheated. He's just being a flirt. He's a flirt. I know that. Besides, Chef Verdi is history. He may never cook again."

"And the world's a better place for it," said Parker.

"True, that." Billy snorted out a laugh. "Want to hear the best part? Turns out that the Japanese Gay Venture Capitalists weren't gay. Something got lost in translation. They meant to say happy or lucky. I think they were a little surprised by the *Queen* and all the references to same-sex relationships. That's what I love about Jeremy. I mean, who else would take a bunch of Japanese bank execs on a tour of P-town's gay bars then feed them tainted whale penis? You have got to admire someone who will do that."

"I'm not sure admiration is what they're feeling as they get their stomachs pumped," I said. "And I still think you ought to look before you leap where Jeremy's concerned."

"I know. I know. You and Harry and Pete and Ella have taken a vote. And you've all decided that I ought to give Parker here a try."

He had me with that. Because it was true. And because I hated having Billy call me on it. It didn't help that Parker was sitting right there next to him.

"Only, you overlooked a few things," said Billy. "The most important being that, despite what the Silva quorum may think, I'm a big boy and I can make my own decisions."

"Bill," I said. He was right. Which was, of course, exactly why I was ready to tell him that he wasn't.

Billy held up a hand, "Let me finish." He stood up and glanced towards the open door that led below decks. "I know what Jeremy is and what he isn't. And I know how you feel about him, that it's a mistake to be with him. But if it's a mistake, it's my mistake and I'm allowed to make it. Besides, Jeremy isn't a bad guy. He's very generous. And I know that he loves me." Billy went over to Parker and put a hand on his shoulder. "Parker, on the other hand, does not love me."

"I like you, Bill," said Parker.

"I like you too, man. As a friend. I don't love you, though. And you don't love me." Billy sat back down and put his hand on my knee. "Parker's not interested in me, Nik. He's got eyes for someone else."

I glanced at Parker, who seemed to be scanning the horizon for incoming frigates. "Really? Is that true?" I asked.

"God, Nik," said Billy. "For a scientist with great powers of observation, you miss the most obvious things." Billy got up and put both hands on Parker's shoulders. "You poor sap," he said, "I should warn you about her," and with that, he went downstairs to tend to Jeremy.

Chapter Forty

Marco

I hadn't wanted to lay down my cards. So Billy had done it for me. Here I thought I was doing such a great job, acting out the part of a gay man. Only a gay man saw right through it. I was transparent as plastic wrap. I might as well have been holding a sign that said Marco and Nikki forever. Or, scratch that, Parker and Nikki forever.

Nikki had given me a look somewhere between contempt and curiosity. A look too hard to read, maybe, but that spelled out disaster none the less. She got up and, without a word to me, followed Billy down the stairs.

So there I was, left on deck, there with the tablecloths all piled in one corner, the bunting half off, the chairs like they'd been caught in a storm. There I was, feeling as big a disaster as that deck. Feeling like maybe I needed an emergency room, some sort of treatment, but I couldn't even name the ailment.

I considered my options. Snatching what little cash I had and getting back on the bus, starting over yet again in Providence or Pittsburgh or Poughkeepsie, some other P-town where I could make up a new story. Play the straight man this time around, because the whole gay act had turned into a fiasco.

I was still contemplating, watching the dark water lick the side of the boat, when Nikki appeared ten minutes later. Her arms crossed, she stared at me, I swear to God I saw her take a deep breath, like she was going to dive over the side rail and test the cold water.

"Let's go," she said finally. And I didn't say no. I didn't say I need to leave. I didn't say goodbye. She said, 'Let's go' and I followed her out to the truck and got in on the passenger side.

She turned left on Bradford. "This isn't the way home," I said. Like I was OnStar and she'd gone the wrong way.

"No," she said, "it's not."

She drove us out to Race Point and we got out. The moon shone over the dunes as Nikki pulled an old quilt out of the chest and started walking towards the beach.

"Where are you going?" I asked, my hand still on the door handle of the truck.

"The beach," she said, giving the obvious answer, as though I'd asked the wrong question.

"Why are you going to the beach?" I asked, walking up behind her.

"Testing a theory," she said, without turning around.

"Most people go to the beach during the day." Nikki had picked up her pace. I was nearly jogging to keep up. She didn't answer, just kept walking. And I kept following.

Thinking I should give it up. Thinking she was impossible. Everyone said she was impossible, and here I was loping after her like a trained dog. Loping after her without so much as an explanation. I can't say I liked the way it made me feel.

After about twenty minutes, Nikki turned and walked up a dune. At the top, she turned again "You coming or not?" she shouted to the wind.

"Not," I shouted back. Thinking it was my last chance to go back to the truck.

"Why not?" And since I couldn't think of a single good reason why not, I trudged up after her. She was sitting cross-legged on the quilt, which she'd spread out in a nest of dune grass. "Warm night," she said, when she saw me.

Then she stood up and walked over to me, put her hands to either side of my face, and kissed me. The kind of kiss that could make a man forget he'd just trudged a mile down a deserted beach for no good reason. The kind of kiss that could make a man forget about anything, could make him forget his name, who he was, and who he was pretending to be. The kind of kiss that cuts through the bullshit to the true. And just when I was in a state of near amnesia, she stopped.

"You're a good kisser for a liar," she said.

"I'm not..." I said, tripping over my tongue.

"You're not what? A good kisser? Or a liar? Or gay?"

"Not gay," I said. "Never gay."

Nikki pulled a foil packet from the pocket of her jeans and held it into the air. "Prove it," she said.

"A condom?" I nearly choked. Of course that's what it was.

"You've got five seconds," she said and she began counting backwards, "five, four..." When she got to zero she tossed the packet as hard as she could into the dune grass. "He who hesitates loses," she said, pulling another foil from her pocket.

I grasped her arm. "Stop it. This is nuts. Just stop."

"Five, four, three..."

I grabbed her hand, closed a fist around the packet, and kissed her. I'm not sure who pulled who down to the blanket. "One, zero," she said softly, letting go her fist.

"This could get out of hand," I said, my lips close to her neck, the warm salt taste of her on my tongue.

"That's what I'm counting on," she whispered back. Shifting to her knees, she pulled off her shirt. She unsnapped my jeans. I let her, let things happen as they would. Isn't this what I'd wanted, after all? Isn't this what I'd wanted ever since the day I'd first laid eyes on her, copper hair blowing in the wind? Life was short. I reached for the condom. She beat me to it.

"First," she said, "I need a few answers."

I was in no condition to take a quiz. "Now?" I said.

"I need to know a guy before I have sex

on the beach with him."

I got up on my knees. "You're impossible."

She came up behind me, her breasts pressing into my back, and kissed my shoulder. "Who are you? Really?" she whispered in my ear. And I knew she had me. There was no going back, no walking away.

"Marco," I said to the dune grass. "My name's Marco."

"Marco Bench?" she said, nipping at my ear lobe.

"Yes, Marco Bench." She backed away and clutched her shirt. "Tornetti," I said. "Marco Tornetti."

Nikki put the shirt down. "Marco Tornetti," she said, as though trying out the name.

"Marco Tornetti," I pulled my hand through her hair. "I'm from New Jersey. I'm a chef." I kissed the space between her breasts, the thump, thump of her heart against my lips telling me she wasn't so calm after all. "And I've never been gay," I said, grabbing the packet that had fallen between us and tearing it open with my teeth.

Chapter Forty One

Nikki

I guess I shouldn't have done it, shouldn't have led Marco to the beach like that. I suppose I could say I didn't know what had gotten into me. But the truth is, I knew exactly what I was doing. It was the outcome that surprised me.

I'd followed Billy below decks and we'd had a furious whispered conversation in which Billy had told me that he was absolutely certain Parker wasn't gay. Said that he could tell just by the way Parker looked at me. Said he didn't know how I'd missed it. And when I said no, that he was wrong, absolutely wrong, Billy had gone into the head and come out with three condoms and dared me to find out for myself.

I was furious at Billy for the assumptions he was making: that I wanted Parker as much as Parker, presumably, wanted me. I was more furious still because I knew the assumptions were right. And I was furious at myself because I wanted, more than anything, for Billy's perceptions about Parker to be true. I went out to the beach to prove Billy wrong. I never thought that Parker would take the bait. I never thought I'd let him take it as easily as I did.

Maybe Ella had been right all along when she joked that I needed to get laid. But no, that was as much a lie as the name Parker Bench. The truth was that we, Marco and I, had been walking toward those dunes ever since he walked into the back of Fishy's T-shirt Hut with a pink flyer and asked about a job. I can't say I'm sorry we walked into those dunes, because as Marco's lips pressed into my neck and his hands began caressing my breasts and traveling south, as we came together with the waves thundering behind us, the world seemed pretty damned close to perfect.

Afterwards, we wrapped ourselves into the quilt-like filling, and Marco stroked my hair and kissed the top of my head. "Why would you lie?" I asked. "About being gay?"

"You sure I was lying?" he teased. Which made me sit up. Because that would have torn it, wouldn't it? Adding gay guy to the short list of men I'd cared about? Gay, married, and celibate, an unholy trinity, that. But Marco laughed and pulled me close. "If we can find that other condom, I'll prove it to you again," he said into my ear.

I nearly told him we didn't have to find it, that I had a spare tucked into my pocket. Then I thought of something else. That, like Ned, Marco still wasn't being totally honest with me.

"You didn't answer my question," I said.

"No. I didn't." He kissed my neck, sending a shiver down my spine, making it clear he had no intention of answering.

"And you don't plan on telling me?" I asked. "What are you hiding from?"

Marco moaned and got up on one elbow. "Let's just say I don't want to be found."

"By whom? Your wife?" I teased. I felt the tension rise in him, the cords of his neck tighten. "Oh my God," I said. "You're married."

"Yes," he said. "But it's not what you think."

"It's not what I think?" I'd already rolled free of the quilt and was pulling on my underwear, putting on my jeans.

"Nikki," Marco called after me as I jogged back down the beach. Make that two married men and a priest. Looks like I'd still hit the triple. "Wait, Nikki," I could hear Marco behind me. I broke into a hard run and was breathless by the time I got to the truck. Marco was still calling my name and asking me to wait.

I didn't wait. I got into the truck and drove off. Walking back into town was small penance for deceiving me yet again. Then, because I'm a sucker for trouble, because in a single night I'd nearly been seduced by Ned and had most definitely been taken in by Marco, I went right over to the guy behind door number three. I drove straight to St. Peter's rectory and rang the bell.

The porch light snapped on and there was Eli tying the cord of his bathrobe and squinting at me. "We've got to talk," I said.

"It's after midnight," he answered.

"I'm aware." We stood gaping at each other for an impossible minute. "You going to let me in?" I asked.

Eli sighed and opened the screen. "Won't you come in? Make yourself at home." The sarcasm wasn't lost on me.

"Thanks." I sat in a club chair. "You got anything to drink?"

Eli blinked at me. "Communion wine? Or whiskey?"

"I was thinking tea."

Eli crossed his arms. "Tea."

"Too late for coffee, don't you think?"

Eli sighed and headed for the kitchen. I followed him and sat at the table while he put the kettle on. "Well? Did you wake me out of a sound sleep so that we could have a tea party?"

"No, I woke you out of a sound sleep for answers," I said. Eli swore under his breath. "You're not supposed to do that," I said.

"It wasn't the Lord's name," he answered.

"Why didn't you tell me about Marco?"

"He told you?"

"His name. That he's from Jersey. And not a whole lot else."

Eli took two cups from the cupboard. "Lemon Zinger or Sleepy Time?"

"Lemon Zinger. Did you know he was married?"

Eli swore again as the tea kettle started to whistle. "What did you do to him?" He made a show of pouring hot water ever so carefully over the bags.

"I left him on the beach." Eli set down the cup and stared at me. "It's a warm night," I said. "The walk will clear his head. Maybe help remind him who he is."

"The walk will clear his head," said Eli, shaking his own head. A sad look passed over his face and he sat down on the chair. "Please tell me you didn't take him there."

"No," I said. "I wouldn't do that."

Nearly twenty years ago, Eli and I had discovered an outermost house on the far reaches of the dune land. Once upon a time, these little shacks had been used as artist's retreats, a place where a writer could make like Thoreau and commune with nature. Eugene O'Neil once had such a shack, as did Norman Mailer. A few of these houses were still in use, but most of them had fallen into disrepair. A number of them were being reclaimed by the elements, as was the case with the little place that Eli and I found. It was a one room shack, the roof was caved in and the single window was hollow, the sea having washed away the pane in some long ago storm. The door was off its hinges and lay on the shanty floor, half buried in the sand that covered the floor like a carpet.

It was Eli who first found the place. He used to take long solitary walks along the beach, which, thinking back on it, may have been a precursor to his being outed by God. He showed the place to me not long after he discovered it and the two of us set to fixing it. We swept away the sand, rehung the door, and covered the empty window with clear plastic sheeting. I bought a rug at the Army-Navy Store and hustled an old quilt from the storage space under the eaves of my bedroom. Eli brought a Coleman lamp and an air mattress, both pilfered from the camping equipment stashed in the Avellar's garage. We lit utility candles stuck in old jars and called the place a honeymoon cottage. Which was fitting, because we spent the spring and early summer of our senior year trysting up there whenever we could sneak away.

For me, the place has always carried the sweetest memory of my soon-to-end childhood days and Eli was there too, I could see it. Only it wasn't the happy parts that Eli was remembering. It was the later parts.

In June of that year, both of us graduated from P-town high. I was valedictorian and the world was my oyster. I knew I wanted a career in oceanography, something related to the family fishing business, which Harry and Pete, one year and three years behind me, would inherit, but not the family business exactly. I loved the idea of studying the depths, had long collected shells and specimens on the beach, and spent long days out on the *Two Sons* with my pop and uncle hauling in nets. I knew the names of all the fish. Oceanography was a natural. I applied to the finest programs in the country. One in Florida and three in California. None nearby. I also applied to Holy Cross, the only school in which Eli was interested. I got accepted everywhere. Eli, applying only to Holy Cross, was accepted there. Both San Diego State and Holy Cross offered me full scholarships, no small thing for the child of a fishing family. I had a choice to make: stay with Eli at Holy Cross or go to San Diego, which had one of the best oceanography programs in the country.

I chose San Diego and broke Eli's heart. The night I told him of my decision, we met at the shack. Eli accused me of not loving him enough, said that he would never go three thousand miles from me. He told me that I was turning away from the best thing that ever happened to either of us. I was young and crazy in love with Eli. But I'd come to realize that I didn't want to follow him to the ends of the earth. I wanted my own journey. The decision tore at me. I hated that Eli wouldn't support me. I told him that he didn't really love me, didn't want my happiness. I told him he was selfish. And I left him in our little beach house and trudged the mile up the beach. I had found the keys to his dad's truck where we'd left them under the floor mat and I drove the six miles back to town, stranding Eli. My *modus operandi* hadn't changed much in the last twenty years.

"I'm sorry I made you walk," I said.

"Yeah, well. I kind of deserved it. You were right. I was a selfish bastard. Maybe I still am."

"I don't think that's true."

Eli smiled, a rueful kind of smile that made me think of what might have been. "It's probably all for the best."

Chapter Forty Two

Marco

I sat on a bench near the empty beach parking lot, pulled off my shoes, and dumped the sand from them. Provincetown was the God-damned sandiest place I'd ever been, the sand in my shoes alone enough to build a sandcastle. It was late and dark and the wind had started coming up off the water like an air conditioner on full blast. I wished I'd worn a jacket. I wished I'd worn socks. But Jesus and Mary, I hadn't come out to Race Point with the intention of a six mile march back into town. I hadn't come out to Race Point with much intention at all, come to think of it.

My head was filled with Nikki Silva. Nikki Silva was the most exasperating woman I'd ever in my life known. I was pissed at being left in the dust. I had lied to her, true. And I had, in watching Nikki Silva with Eli and with Thor, known that she wasn't as unbreakable as she led on. She had a tenderness that she worked hard to cover. She'd uncovered it back in those dunes and I'd thought myself the luckiest son of a bitch on God's earth.

Jesus and Mary, I would have promised her anything up in those dunes and I would have meant to keep those promises. I sat on the bench a long time feeling damned sorry for myself. Then I told myself that six miles was a long way and if I wanted to get to town by sunrise, I'd better get a move on. I picked my sorry self up off the bench and started putting one foot in front of the other. I hadn't gotten far beyond the lot when a truck pulled up on the shoulder in front of me. My first thought was that Nikki had come back. Half of me wanted to get into the truck with her and the other half wanted to say, "Forget about it, I'll take my chances on the road."

The window rolled down and there in the driver's seat sat Eli. "Need a ride?" he asked.

I wasn't too happy to see the good Father at that moment, but a ride's a ride and I got in so as to save my dogs from heel blisters.

"Out cruising?" I asked.

"Out to find you." Eli put the truck into drive and started back towards the beach. "Nik came to see me," he said, pulling into a spot near the bench I'd just deserted.

"So you're what, going to tag team me? Raise my hopes then kick me in the nads and drive off?"

"Is that what she did?" Eli asked, getting out of the truck. He climbed to the top of the dune and stood there, his hair blowing in the wind, looking like some forlorn guy from one of those old Gothic movies.

"You can't see it from here," he said, when I walked up next to him, "but down there somewhere just past that last dune is an outer-most house. A little cabin, probably fallen in on itself by now. Nik and I used to go there when we were kids."

"I thought you were the one supposed to hear confessions."

Eli gave me a look that said shut up and listen already. I knew he hadn't come all the way out to Race Point to tell me about his and Nik's teenaged passion. Besides, I'd already figured that part out. As any fool would have.

"She left me on the beach," he said. "We had this nasty fight and she stormed off in my dad's car. I was fit to be tied. We were so mad at each other that we didn't talk for a week. Then she left for school in California and that turned out to be the last time we saw each other for twenty years. It wasn't a pretty place to leave things."

"You had a right to be pissed. She left you."

"I wasn't blameless. Oh, I thought I was. But twenty years gives you some perspective. I should have swallowed my pride. I should have talked to her. I regret that to this day."

"So what, then you would have made nice and you'd be married to Nik instead of being a priest?"

"No, Marco. Nik and I were destined to go our separate ways. We both knew it and didn't want to admit it. It would have been nice if something so good hadn't ended so badly." He turned to me again. "I don't even know why I'm telling you all this. I think you might be trouble, but Nik, let's just say she doesn't get angry without good reason. She's angry because you hurt her. And I don't want to see her hurt."

"So I ought to what, swallow my pride and go tell her I'm sorry she left me on the beach?"

"She had her reasons. And you've got a choice to make."

"Walk away or figure out how to stay?"

"Something like that." Eli began walking down the dune. Halfway down, he turned. "Oh, and Marco? You hurt that woman any more than you already have and it won't be the mob you've got to worry about."

Eli dropped me off at the Silvas'. I can't say that his little talk had done much to clear my head. And I can't say I was feeling so hot after having been deserted by the one woman I gave a damn about, then being threatened by a priest who cared about her too.

Damnedest part of the whole deal was that I knew Eli was right. When I looked at it from Nikki's perspective, I'd have left me on the beach too. She'd been nothing but straight with me. She'd taken me in. I'd lied to her and she'd let me do it.

Now that Nikki knew the truth, or part of the truth, anyway, it would probably be best if I made like John Wayne and rode off into the sunset. Or the sunrise on the 5:00 a.m. bus to points north of here. Thing was, I didn't want to go. Nick was after me to stay and do the flea market thing. There was this big jumble sale at the Blessing of the Fleet, which was this big deal celebration coming up next month. Harry and Pete were carrying a statue of St. Peter on the *Two Sons*, that was, to Nick's way of thinking, one of the greatest honors ever bestowed on his family.

So, there was the blessing, and there was Billy, who Nick had finally started talking to again. Billy said that had to do with me, because I spent a lot of time chatting Billy up to his pop. Truth was, Nick loved his youngest kid. Like his daughter, Nick wasn't as tough as he wanted everyone to believe. But if I could get Nick to take Billy back and maybe even to accept Jeremy, well, I owed that much to Billy.

Like Eli said, I had choices to make. Stay and try and make things work. Or leave, before things got any more heated. It was practically the next morning and I figured I owed it to myself to sleep on it. I was half-past tired as I made my way up the porch steps, unlocked the door, and made my way up the stairs, nearly tripping over Nick's cat as I climbed. And nearly falling down the stairs when I reached the top and had a run-in with a big, black Samsonite bag parked at the head of the stairs. Lucky for me, the bag was empty, so I didn't break the toe I'd stubbed on it.

I swore under my breath so as not to wake up the whole neighborhood and dragged the suitcase into my room. There was a post-it note stuck to the top of it. "Goodbye Marco," it said. And in that moment, tired or no, sleepy or no, I made up my mind. I wasn't that easy to get rid of. You couldn't just take me to a deserted beach, have your way with me, then shove me aside. I knew how dumb that sounded, even to myself. But the beach made me think about how Nik kissed me, how she might as well have set fire to me. How her shoulders, Jesus, her shoulders were soft.

I marched across the hall and made like to knock and changed my mind again. No knocking, I decided. We were past knocking. I barged into the room.

Nikki was lying on the narrow bed she had under the eaves, facing the window that looked out over the side yard. She didn't turn, but she had an arm propped under her head and I could tell she wasn't sleeping.

"You are the most exasperating, the most difficult, the most hotheaded woman I've ever in my life had the chance to meet," I said. I noticed it then. How her shoulders had the slightest shiver to them. A tiny sigh came from the bed.

"You're crying," I said. Dumb, I know. But I wasn't really sure what it was I was supposed to do.

Nikki shook her head.

"You are too crying," I said. I went over to the bed and put my hand on her shoulder, my own eyes kind of getting loaded up.

"Don't," she said. Which made me reach down and kiss the shoulder. "Don't cry," I said.

"I'm not," she said.

"You are too, you sound all nasally."

"Maybe I'm allergic to you," she said.

Chapter Forty Three

Nikki

I hate crying. I know, crying is supposed to be this weapon that women use to make men all weak-kneed and crazy. It's never worked that way for me. My brothers would never have been swayed by my tears. I was the oldest of the Silva kids, the toughest. And I was a girl, which was all the more reason to tough it out. I've always toughed it out. I cried over Eli and I cried over Ned, but never in front of them. Not once in front of them. And here I was, barely able to catch my voice, my nose gone snotty and my eyes like peeled eggs. And over what? Some married Jersey boy who didn't know the stern from the bow? Who had lied to me since the day we'd met?

I wiped my eyes on the sheet and grabbed a Kleenex. Then I told Marco Tornetti that I didn't need any more complications in my life, thanks anyway. My life had a way of blowing up, literally and figuratively, and the last thing I needed was a relationship with a married man who used an alias and pretended he was gay.

"Too late," he said. "You and I already have a relationship."

"Had," I said. "It's over."

"I said I was sorry. I am sorry. I shouldn't have lied to you."

"Lied?" I got to my feet. "How about still lying? Present tense, Marco. I have no idea who you are."

"You know exactly who I am," he said, "in all the ways that count."

"What is that supposed to mean?" I crossed my arms. "Jesus, and you think I'm exasperating."

Marco walked over to me, took my arms, uncrossed them, and looked into my eyes. God, he had nice eyes. "You are exasperating," he said. "You're exasperating and smart and drop-dead gorgeous. And I..."

I pulled away. "And you what? Think it's okay to lead me on?"

"I never led you on. I lied, yes, but I never led you on."

"You told me you were gay. You told me you were from Canada. You told me you were a fisherman."

"And you never believed any of it. Except the gay thing. You believed the gay thing. Which is real ironic, because that's the one thing I'd of wished you hadn't believed."

"You didn't tell me you were married. Were you going to let me in on that? God knows what else you've lied about."

"I didn't tell you because I was trying to protect you."

"From what?"

"Sharks," he said, "really big sharks."

He was getting as cryptic as Eli. I wasn't having it. Not anymore. "What are you talking about?"

"You ever hear of John Gotti?"

"The Mafia guy?"

"New York mob. Runs all kinds of rackets in Jersey, too. He's got a lieutenant by the name of Fat Phil Lezario."

"Fat Phil?" I might have smirked a little. A picture of a fat shark in a gangster suit popped into my head.

"Not funny," said Marco. "My wife, Lark? She's Fat Phil's daughter."

"Lark? Your wife's name is Lark. Lark and Parker Bench. Very nice."

"Again, not funny." Then Marco sat on the bed and told me the whole story. And by the time he finished, I wasn't laughing anymore.

Chapter Forty Four

Marco

Nikki stared at me with a little bit of fear and a whole lot of concern and maybe just a pinch of something else. The something else erased any doubt I may have had. Woman cared about me for real.

Of course, I knew she cared. I knew that she wasn't just playing me on the beach. Nikki on the beach might have been angry and a little confused, but she was tender. She made love like a woman in love. I've been around. I know the difference between the real thing and going through the motions. On the beach, that was the real thing. I knew it then. But the way she looked at me after I told her everything, I would have bet my life on it. I *was* betting my life on it. And, with a terrible sense of dread, I knew I may be betting her life on it, too.

"So these people, this Phil, is looking for you?" she asked.

"I don't know. I've been trying to figure it all out. I'm pretty sure that Lark married me because she was trying to cover her ass. She was into all kinds of kinky shit and she didn't want Daddy to know. So I was her patsy, dumb enough to take the fall. As for Phil, leaving Newark was the only thing I could have done. I couldn't have stayed to find out what Phil's next move would be." I looked her in the eye. "You get how serious..."

"I get it. A person doesn't up and leave without so much as a wallet without some strong motivation."

"Yeah," I said. "That's true. The thing is, I didn't think about where I was going. Only why. And what I found," I ran my finger down Nikki's cheek, "is so much better than what I left behind. I don't want to leave you. Not when I just found you."

Nikki didn't say anything for a long time, then she put her hands to my face and she kissed me. Jesus and Mary, she kissed me and you'd have thought I'd never been with a woman before. You'd have thought it was the first time. When we finally pulled away, her hands still a warm imprint on my face, her eyes were wet. "Then stay."

Chapter Forty Five

Nikki

It was hard to imagine what sort of a future Marco and I could have. A future built on deception, a tenuous house of cards, that. A future we seemed destined towards anyway. We talked a lot in that May and June. Talked of marriages and sharks and relationships. I kept Marco's secret, kept calling him Parker, kept pretending he was gay.

It wasn't hard to do. The Blessing of the Fleet was only a few weeks away. The blessing, and the Portuguese festival that runs alongside it, is a big deal in the P-town fishing community. In my family, it's an annual event that is at least as important as Christmas and that far outshines any of the lesser holidays.

Even when I was in California, I always made an effort to be home for the blessing. Ned used to scoff at the whole affair. He couldn't understand why I'd travel several thousand miles for a hokey town event that included parading a statue of St. Peter up and down the streets in the arms of men dressed in traditional costumes. He could never understand how the blessing, all of its carnival splendor dressed in a religious cloak, was an integral part of who I was. Because, deep down under the oceanographic degree and the research grants, I was still the

Portuguese-American daughter of a fisherman. Ned, in his breezy, California way, was immune to such things as tradition.

Parker, on the other hand, seemed to revel in it. He loved the whole notion of it, said it reminded him of the Italian neighborhood he'd grown up in. "We paraded a statue of the Virgin Mary," he said, "and ate large amounts of macaroni with Sunday gravy." He helped Harry and Pete scrub the *Two Sons* stem to stern and to decorate her mast with hundreds of colored flags.

The *Two Sons* had the distinguished honor of leading the blessing parade with St. Peter propped in his flowered arbor like a masthead at the bow. When I was a girl, there were twenty or more fishing families in P-town. Economic realities and the hardships of fishing had dwindled that number to ten. Twenty or ten, we were a tight group, a community. And the honor of leading the fleet and representing that community was not taken lightly by anyone in my family.

We all got in on the act. Ella volunteered to make two tons of salad for the Friday night barbeque. Viddie smothered the altar at St. Peter's in carnations and lilies. My brothers scrubbed the boat. I made a run to a Plymouth butcher for what was said to be the best linguica sausage in eastern Massachusetts.

The bishop was coming from Fall River to preside over the blessing and staying at the rectory at St. Peter's. Eli, hosting the bishop for the first time and also charged with presiding over two Masses, leading the parade, and arranging the details of the blessing itself, bustled between the Altar Society and the harbor master's office and the barbeque committee as though he were born to the task. And, though considering our history it was hard for me to admit, I saw in Eli a man finally comfortable in his own skin.

Amid all that preparation it was easy to forget that Parker wasn't Parker. Easy to forget that he might still consider leaving.

Chapter Forty Six

Marco

The festival took up everyone's time and energy and made it easy to forget my personal trouble. Maybe it was nostalgia, but I loved the whole idea. Like I'd told Nikki, it reminded me of where I grew up. Every year, in August, there was a Feast of the Assumption, complete with a statue and a parade and a lot of food.

"My uncle Sal would play the accordion," I said. I was sitting on the bed in my room at the Silvas', watching Nikki root around in the crawl space that ran along the eaves for the length of the room.

"That sounds about right." Nikki crawled into the space and only the backs of her sneakers were visible. "We've got quite a few musicians. Rusty Cook plays a mean mandolin." Nikki sneezed and backed out of the crawl space sliding two cardboard boxes stacked one atop the other. The larger of the two was sealed shut. "Good God, he's hiding his stash," she said, grabbing a pair of scissors and running them through the packing tape.

"Always a little like Christmas with your father's packages."

Nikki didn't crack a smile. "He has got

to stop this," she said, pulling a stainless steel cooking pot from the box.

I took the pot from her, nearly spraining my wrist it was that heavy, and turned it over. "Regalware," I said. "This is quality stuff."

"I'm going to have to another talk with him," Nikki said.

Talking, in Nick and Nik terms, usually meant shouting and gesticulating until one or the other of them stomped off. Last thing I needed was Nikki, in a fit of anger, spouting off about me. I did my best diversion tactic. "What's in the other box?"

"Costumes," she said, distracted by the bait. Momentarily, at least. She flipped the top open and pulled out two vests, one gold, one crimson, and held up the crimson one. "Pop got this from my grandfather." She laid the vest on the bed and pulled out a multicolored skirt and a white ruffled blouse. "And my mom, she got this from her grandmother. There's an apron that goes with it. And these." Nikki held up a pair of lacy white leggings."

"These will look hot on you," I said, taking the leggings from her.

"I've never worn this," she said.

"Why not?"

Nik fingered the blouse's pearl buttons. "I guess I never thought I could fill it out right."

"You can fill it out fine," I said, kissing her ear. "And I'm not speaking in the physical."

Half an hour later I was down in the kitchen getting the recipe for Portuguese Kale Soup from Nick. Bill and Jeremy had offered up the newly finished kitchen at the Red Tomato for festival preparation and I'd offered to make a big pot of the soup in the new kitchen.

"Can I borrow the Regalware?" I asked Nick.

"What Regalware?"

"The pots in the box upstairs. Nikki found them."

"Oh, for the love of St. Pete," said Nick. "She's going to give me what for, isn't she?"

"They're good pots. Restaurant quality."

"That's what the guy on QVC said. Restaurant quality for sixty-nine dollars and ninety-five cents."

"No kidding? Sixty-nine ninety-five? Those pots are worth twice that." I might not know much, but I know from pots and pans.

"It was a closeout deal. I was going to sell them at the jumble sale on Saturday. You really think I can get maybe a hundred bucks for the set?"

"Easy money. Anybody who knows pots will know that's a bargain."

"Maybe I should order up a couple more sets."

"No ordering," said Nikki from the hall. "I'm confiscating your credit card."

Nick opened his mouth to say something and left it hanging open.

Because Nikki had come into the kitchen wearing her mother's costume. "Pop?" Nikki asked, as Nick sank into a kitchen chair. "You okay?"

"Fine," he said, staring at his daughter.

"I'll take it off." Nikki said, moving back toward the door.

"You wearing it in the parade?" Nick asked.

"I was thinking about it. Ella wears her grandmother's and I..."

"You wear it."

"You sure?"

"'Course I'm sure. You wear it." Nick swallowed. "You look just like your mother."

"She's something," I said, after Nikki had gone.

"You can use the pots," Nick said. "Since it's for a good cause. I'll order some more." He looked at me kind of funny. "She's a good girl, my Nikki. Too bad you aren't interested."

I understood it, the look. I don't know how long he'd known or if Nikki and I weren't as good at keeping secrets as I'd thought. But Nick Silva had it figured.

Chapter Forty Seven

Nikki

Besides the linguica we needed vegetables for the soup and Marco insisted that they be fresh. We spent an hour at the Stop & Shop as Marco fingered kale, sniffed cabbages, and weighed potatoes in his hands. We took the coveted findings over to the Red Tomato. We got out in front of the dilapidated building and Marco walked over to the spot where the roof was caved in. "Skylight?" he asked.

"You've seen the plans."

"They really expected to open this place a week ago?"

"Might have worked if the Japanese had come through. Damn that whale penis." We walked inside.

"That is a nice bar." Marco ran his hand along the wood grain. "Solid oak. Plank floors, too."

"You sound like Jeremy."

"Let's hope the kitchen has running water," he said. Jeremy had assured us that the kitchen was state of the art. But considering the state of the dining room, it was hard to think he wasn't exaggerating. "Holy macaroni." Marco held the swinging door and stared.

"What?" I asked, coming up behind him.

"This is unbelievable." Marco's eyes lit like birthday candles as he surveyed the stainless steel countertops, the industrial sink, the stainless refrigerator. Jeremy, it seems, had not been exaggerating.

"Vulcan," said Marco, running his hands along the ten burner stove. "This is a Vulcan. They're custom made."

"That must be why Jeremy and Billy ran out of funds after the kitchen remodel."

"A Vulcan. I've always wanted to cook on a Vulcan."

"Guess some dreams do come true."

Marco ignored my comment and began playing with burners. "Huge grill top," he said. "We have to go back to the store."

I eyed the grocery bags. We already had enough ingredients to make soup for the entire population of Portugal and he wanted to get more?

"Because I need to...soup is a start, but you can't use a kitchen like this and just make Portuguese Kale Soup. I want to do a bouillabaisse. Two kinds of soup are better than one, right? And I'll make us some dinner. Veal chops, maybe. We'll bring them home to Nick, surprise him. You like veal chops, right? Or maybe a veal roast? Or a rack of lamb? Or..."

"Stop," I said, putting my fingers to his lips. "You are here to make soup, not design a menu."

"But I could," he said, taking my wrist.

"I could. Jesus and Mary, what I could do with this kitchen."

I'd never seen him so excited. I understood the impulse; I felt the same way about unlocking the mysteries of migration. To each his own. Still, we didn't have the money to spring for a feast. I told Marco as much.

"Maybe I should play the lottery," said Marco, rinsing out my pop's new pot.

"Who's playing the lottery?" asked Billy, walking into the kitchen.

Marco went over and put his arm around Bill's shoulder. "Do you have any friggin' idea how great this kitchen is?"

"Does he always get this excited?" Billy asked me.

"Only around cookware," I said.

Marco ignored both of us. "This kitchen. It's state of the art."

"You sound like Jeremy," Billy said. We began unpacking the groceries.

"He's a chef," I said.

"You're straight and you're a chef." Billy pulled a cabbage from the bag. "What else are you keeping from us?"

Marco filled the stockpot with water and threw in the beans without answering.

"She's not kidding, is she?" Billy said. "You really are a chef. You're a chef and you let us go through the Verdi disaster?" He pointed to the walk-in freezer. "We still have about two tons of whale clogging up the works."

"I know," I said. "I don't know what to do with it."

"We're not using it in the bouillabaisse,"

261

said Marco. "I think we've learned that lesson."

"What bouillabaisse?" said Jeremy, coming in through the swinging door and inspecting the cabbages we'd laid on the counter.

"Parker wants to make bouillabaisse," Billy said. "Lots here Parker didn't tell us. He's a chef. And he's not gay, either."

Jeremy gave Parker a once-over. "Are you sure?" he asked.

"About the gay part or the chef part?" Parker asked.

"Both."

"He's really good in the kitchen," I said.

Billy eyed me. "And elsewhere, too," he said. I hurled a cabbage at him; he ducked.

"Nikki and Parker?" asked Jeremy. "Well, stuff me with chestnuts and call me a Thanksgiving turkey."

"Do not," I picked up the cabbage and aimed at Jeremy's head. "start blabbing about that."

"Quit abusing my cabbage," said Marco, taking the cabbage from me.

"Is that what she's doing?" Jeremy asked.

"Seriously, though," said Billy. "Why all the secrecy?"

"I can't tell you that," Marco said.

"Because if he told us he'd have to kill us," Jeremy said.

"If he doesn't tell us, I don't think he can use our kitchen," Billy said.

"I don't know. He did say something

about bouillabaisse."

"And veal chops," Marco said.

"And veal chops," said Jeremy. "Bless his lying little heart if he can cook me a veal chop."

Marco ran his hand along the restaurant-quality grill top. "The things I could do with this grill."

Chapter Forty Eight

Marco

"You can't." Nikki took my hand from the grill. It felt as though she'd slapped me in the face. Trying to slap some sense into me, I guess you could have said. But I was feeling pretty sensible. It was all clear to me now. I didn't have to live this lie. It was wrong to lie to the people I cared about. And I did care about them, about Nik and Billy and the rest of her family. I even cared about Jeremy. They had no idea who Fat Phil was, he belonged to another life, a life that wouldn't catch up to me here. I had this life, a life that served up a Vulcan stove and shiny appliances and virgin countertops.

"I think we can trust them," I said.

"Are you insane? Jeremy couldn't keep a secret if his life depended on it."

"Excuse me," said Jeremy. "Jeremy's here, present in the room. And I can, too, keep a secret."

"No, you can't," said Nikki. "You're a blabber."

"I am not a blabber. I do not blab. I might gush on occasion, but I do not blab."

"He does not blab," said Billy. "We dated for six months before I came out of the

264

closet."

"You what?" Nikki looked at her brother. "You told me you'd just met Jeremy when you introduced him to me."

"Like I said, he doesn't blab."

"And don't think it was easy, girlfriend, keeping a man like Billy under wraps in a place like P-town. But I promised him we'd go slowly, give him a chance to get the *familia* used to his being gay."

"Wow," said Nikki. "I'm not sure if I should hug you or punch your lights out."

"Tit for tat," said Jeremy. "You are not the only one who can keep a secret."

"The two of you need to quit it," I said. "And personally, I'm a little tired of all the secret keeping." It was my secret to keep or not, so I told them, all about Fat Phil and Vlad and the gnocchi. I even told them about Lark.

"You poor boy," said Jeremy. "No wonder you're so stressed. I thought it was just because you worked for Nicola."

"What is that supposed to mean?" Nikki asked.

"You can be a little bitchy, darling,"

"I can be a little bitchy? You are a flaming, flirting fruit who probably cheats on my brother, and I can be a little bitchy?"

"Enough, Nik," said Billy, the minute before I could spit it out of my mouth.

"I never cheated on Billy. Ever. I like to flirt, true. But I never cheated. You, on the other hand, blew up a boat and a whale."

"I never blew up anything. Ever. You poisoned a boatload of unsuspecting business men."

"I did not."

"Quit it, both of you," I said. "Nik, say you're sorry for calling Jeremy a cheat."

"But..."

"No buts. He would never have bought the *Queen* if you hadn't needed a boat. Isn't that true, Jeremy?"

"Well, I suppose that maybe..."

"And who went to bat for us with Pop?" said Billy. "Nikki stood up for us and you know it."

"I should have done more," said Nik. We all looked at her. "I should have...moved out or something, until Pop talked to Bill."

"But Pop did talk to me. And your being on my side, that meant a lot, Nik. That meant everything." Bill gave Nik a hug, then Jeremy came over and the three of them were huddled together and I was wondering if maybe I should just go when Bill said, "Get over here," and I joined the huddle, too.

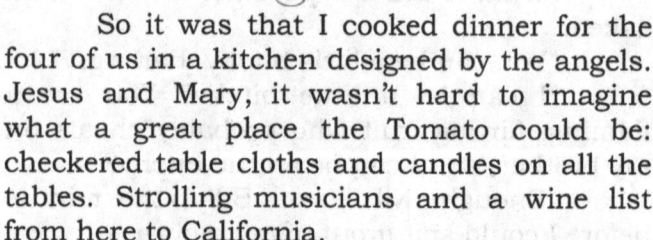

So it was that I cooked dinner for the four of us in a kitchen designed by the angels. Jesus and Mary, it wasn't hard to imagine what a great place the Tomato could be: checkered table cloths and candles on all the tables. Strolling musicians and a wine list from here to California.

"Amazing," said Jeremy, taking a bite of veal chop. "This is food fit for the gods. You," he pointed a fork at me, "are a genius. And the new chef at the Red Tomato. If you'll have us."

"Only one problem," Billy said.

"What's that?" Jeremy asked.

"Look around you," Nik said.

"I know it needs work," Jeremy said.

"And you have no funds."

"Funds come and funds go," said Jeremy. "Sooner or later the universe will provide us with a way to make this place happen. It's already provided us with a chef."

Nik shook her head. "You really believe you can will the Tomato to happen?"

"It worked for you, sis. You wanted to do research and Jeremy willed you a boat and an assistant."

"And look how that turned out," Nikki said.

"Should I be insulted?" I asked.

"No," said Nikki. "I was talking about the research part."

"Maybe the universe isn't done with you yet," said Jeremy. "And don't under estimate the romance part."

Nikki's smile could tackle anything the universe put in her way. "You're right," she said. "I guess some things do work out."

Chapter Forty Nine

Nikki

Jeremy was still the biggest queen in all of P-town, which is saying something, but it was clear by the way that he looked at my brother that he really did care about Billy. And he really did want the Tomato to work.

"You could sell the boat," I said, "and raise funds that way."

"I couldn't sell the boat. How would you do your research?"

"What research?" I said. "There is no more research."

"There is always research," said Jeremy, "and you must do it. You would be lost without your work."

"I'm hardly lost," I said. "I have you guys. And the rest of the family. And Parker. That's what matters."

Marco began to clear the table and, telling Jeremy and Billy to stay where they were, I followed him into the kitchen.

"What?" I asked.

"That was nice, what you said about family. And me."

"And?"

"And I love you, Nikki. I'm a guy so stupid that I thought a mobster would give me a fair shake. And you're a beautiful woman, the smartest damned woman I've ever known. I love you and I have no right to."

I'd loved two men before Marco. And neither of them had ever made me feel like I did at that moment. Cherished, special. "You have every right," I said. "Because I love you, too."

The festival began the next day. Marco got up at dawn and went to the Tomato's kitchen. By nine, he had a vat of Portuguese Kale Soup, which was a good thing because it seemed as though every Portuguese American east of the Hudson had converged on our little town. The place was alive with costumes and bands and dancing troupes' stomping feet.

We took the soup to Ella's and she dipped a spoon into the cold soup and tasted. Better than her grandmother's, she declared, to which Marco said it would be even better warmed.

Ella's place began to fill as Marco and I sat in a corner booth tackling the two by two special: two eggs, two strips of bacon, two slices of buttered toast. We were halfway through coffee refills when the door jangled and in walked a man tall as he was wide, a bowling ball head propped on his shoulders looking as though it would roll off as there was no neck to fasten it to.

He was wearing a sports shirt, arms nearly bursting from the sleeves like bowling pins to complete the theme. Yet I might not have noted the man at all, might have given him a glance and pegged him as just another tourist come to Ella's for a pre-festival breakfast had Marco not gone pasty. With a hard clank, he dropped the spoon he'd been using to sugar his coffee, took the hood of the sweatshirt he was wearing, and pulled it up over his face in a bad imitation of a rapper.

"Good Christ, that's Angelo," he whispered, when I asked him what he thought he was doing. "What's he doing here?"

It was a rhetorical question, of course. I had no idea why the bowling ball man was in town. Marco turned his head towards the wall. "What's he doing?"

"What's who doing?"

"The guy with the big head. Angelo. What's he doing?"

"Talking to Ella," I said.

"Oh, Jesus and Mary."

"Relax. He probably wants breakfast. That's what most people come in here for."

Ella seated the big guy, Angelo, at the counter, his back to us. Marco wondered aloud if we could get by him. "Can we go out the back?"

"Through the kitchen?" I asked.

"Yes." Marco left his half-eaten toast on the table, pulled the hood farther over his head, and headed for the kitchen door. Ella raised her eyebrows at me as I followed, but follow I did.

It didn't take Marco long to pack. "I'm sorry," he said, as he threw a few shirts, and several pairs of workpants into the suitcase I'd left on the stairs for him that fateful night a few weeks back. I was upset at Marco's sudden goodbye. He told me, once we got out to the dumpsters behind Ella's, all his reasons.

It seemed Angelo had worked with Marco in the kitchens of Roma's. But, Marco had long suspected, given that Angelo had no particular talent as a cook or even as a dishwasher, that his real talents lay elsewhere. Angelo, it seemed, was one of Fat Phil's henchman. A guy called in to break your legs or your neck if Fat Phil took a dislike to you.

I didn't want no-neck Angelo to break Marco's neck, so I could see his need to hitch a ride on the next bus out of town. And yet. "Maybe you're wrong," I said as Marco threw four pairs of balled socks into the suitcase. "Maybe he's here on vacation. Maybe he's Portuguese."

Marco closed the case and put his arms around me. "I don't like this any better than you do," he said. "But I don't have a choice."

It occurred to me that he did have choices. He could run from one town to the next, from one menial job to the next, or he could stay and see things through. I told him as much. "Sooner or later, you have to stop running," I said.

We heard footsteps on the stairs and Marco moved away from me just as Pop poked his head in the door. He held up the jackets, encased in plastic wrap. "Picked these up from the dry cleaners just now." He handed them to Marco. "There's one for you in there. Yours if you want to be a Silva this weekend."

I bit the inside of my cheek to let the remark go by. Pop noticed.

"You two have a falling out?" Pop pointed to the suitcase. "What's this?"

"Parker's leaving," I said.

"You're what?" Pop asked.

"I'm leaving."

"For the love of St. Joe, why?"

"Because he's a coward," I said.

"I am not a coward. I just... I have to..." Marco wouldn't look at my father.

"What? You having an identity crisis? You think you're gay but any fool can see you have feelings for my little girl. And I'm thinking, this is a good thing. You're a nice boy. A little mushy, but a good kid. I like you. Nikki likes you. God knows she needs someone to look out for her. But I guess I was wrong about you. You decided to be gay."

"I didn't decide, Nick. No one decides," Marco had raised his voice. I'd never heard him raise his voice before. "I never was gay. And I'm in love with your daughter. But that doesn't change a damned thing."

"I knew it!" said Pop. "I knew you weren't gay. No gay guy looks at a woman the way you look at my Nikki. I knew it!"

"Pop," I said, "don't."

Chapter Fifty

Marco

It was maybe the worst moment of my whole life, when Nick stormed out of that room, saying I could forget about the jacket, forget about being an honorary Silva, forget about all of it, and just go, already. Nikki gave me a long, hard look and followed her father down the stairs.

I picked up the suitcase, not very heavy. Jesus and Mary, I had next to nothing and I was leaving what I had, for what? For the first time in my life since my Nona died I had people who cared about me. And I was going to throw it all away for Fat Phil. Maybe Nikki was right. Maybe I was a coward. Maybe some things were worth the fight. I put down the suitcase and went downstairs.

Nick sat in the recliner, Nikki on the couch, the two of them staring at a game show that neither was watching. I went and switched off the TV. "You're right," I said to Nikki. "I don't want to go. Maybe I don't have to." Then I told Nick all about the trouble I was in. "Thing is," I said. "I still got a hit man after me."

"Hells bells," said Nick. "You know how many people come to town for the Blessing? You know what they say about numbers.

273

You'll be hiding in plain sight. We find this Angelo and we keep an eye on him."

"What if he sees us?"

"We see him first."

"I don't know."

"I haven't missed a parade in sixty years and I'm not about to miss one because of some gangster," said Nick. "And if I'm in the parade, you're in the parade because I went and dry cleaned two jackets and I can't wear the both of them."

We heard a "Yoo hoo!" from Viddie at the kitchen door. The woman had a way with timing, I got to say, and none of it good.

"What does she want now?" said Nick under his breath.

"I'll go see." Nikki looked relieved at the excuse to get out of the room. She came back in ten minutes later carrying a purple box wrapped in ribbon. "You are not going to believe this," she said.

"Your birthday isn't till November," said Nick, as I took the box from her.

"Not a birthday present," Nikki said. I untied the ribbon and opened the flap. Inside, cushioned in white tissue paper was what must have been the biggest dildo on sale in all of P-town. A small card, with a tasteful logo of a purple figure dancing, said "Good Vibrations" in a fancy script.

"Why is Viddie giving you a dildo?" I asked.

"It's not for me, it's for Pop," Nikki said. Nick, who had gone slightly pink at the mention of a dildo, went scarlet at the mention of his name. "She wants him to display it at the jumble sale. Thinks it's a good way to drum up business for Tripp."

Nick's mouth hung halfway down his neck, but he recovered enough to say, "Well, that just seals it. Viddie Snow has officially climbed onto the crazy bus."

"She's been on that bus a long, long time. She must be halfway to California by now," Nikki said, and her father started to laugh.

"Viddie Snow. My sister Viddie, proud member of the Rosary Society and expert on all things good and evil," he shook his head. "I always knew she had a blind spot for that kid of hers, but this takes the cake."

Nikki had, in the meanwhile, taken the card from the fancy box.

"Introducing the Bolero," she read.

"The Bolero?" I said, taking the device from the tissue paper.

"Put that thing away," Nick said.

"Why? You afraid it will explode?" Nikki asked.

"Exploding dildo," I said. "That might come in handy against the likes of Angelo." I took the dildo and pointed it at her.

"Put that away before somebody gets hurt," Nick had gotten up out of his recliner. "I'm going over to Viddie's tell her what's what. She wants to display sex toys, let her get her own table over to the jumble."

But the dildo had given me an idea. "Okay if I borrow this?" I said.

"Excuse me?" Nikki asked.

"Not that." And I told her my idea, that if I put the thing in my jacket pocket it might just look like I was packing. Which might work to deter Angelo.

"Packing." Nikki rolled her eyes.

"You got a better idea?" I asked.

Chapter Fifty One

Nikki

We got through two days of festivity without one Angelo Del Rossi sighting. It wasn't for lack of trying. Marco was jumpy as a cat on uppers. He saw hit men sitting on benches, hit men on the trolley bus tour, hit men chatting on the Post Office steps. All of P-town's male inhabitants began, in Marco's eyes, to look like Angelo. At least from a distance.

Marco fingered the dildo he'd stuffed in his jacket pocket and said, "Don't look, but I think that's him walking down the pier." And I'd look and say, "The guy with the ice cream cone? Not him unless he's taken to dressing in drag."

All that anxiety wears on a person, and by Sunday I was nearly as jumpy as Marco. Safety in numbers, Pop reminded us as we lined for up for the procession. Marco took it one step further by falling in between Rusty Cook and Joey Dyer, both of whom had been linebackers for the P-town high football team once upon a time, and both of whom had since that time increased their considerable girth.

"Don't look," whispered Marco, as I

marched in front of him. I decided, for my sanity and his, that it was best to ignore these outbursts. For all we knew, Angelo was on his way back to a life of crime in New Jersey. I pretended not to hear. Which was easy, considering that the contingent marching just behind us, from the Dover Portuguese American Society, included several accordion players and a man hammering on a set of snare drums.

Marco, not easily dissuaded, tapped me on the shoulder. "Quite a crowd," I said to Ella, who marched beside me. "They must be four deep." The crowd on Commercial Street was indeed four deep, nearly outnumbering the crowd in the procession itself. Ella nodded. I felt a tug on my shoulders as Marco maneuvered the two of us out of the procession to the sidewalk.

"That's him," Marco said.

"That's a statue of St. Peter," I said, because it seemed as though Marco was nodding in the direction of the statue being held aloft by four of St. Peter's parishioners.

"Not him. Him," said Marco. "Across the street."

I was just about to inform him that neither of the two men holding hands looked remotely like Angelo, when I saw. "That is him."

"Are you sure?" Marco asked.

"Yes. I'm sure."

"Jesus and Mary."

"Safety in numbers," I said, as much to reassure myself as him.

"Right. In this crowd, no one will see

who fired the shots."

"I don't think he's spotted us," I said. Indeed, Angelo seemed to be watching the strolling guitarists who were passing along the route. After which, he looked at his watch and began weaving through the crowd in the opposite direction from the pier and the procession. "He's leaving," I said, feeling relieved.

"We've got to follow him."

"What?"

"If we know where he is, he can't find us."

Chalk it up to anxiety, but this idea rang with a strange sort of perverted logic. Marco and I began weaving through the crowd on our side of the street. We followed Angelo for a block and saw as he turned into an alley near the Post Office. We managed to cross the street, tangling briefly with a group of Portuguese dancers and followed him down the narrow alley. "Heavenly Hamburgers," said Marco as we watched him. "How can he eat at a time like this?"

Marco and I stood against the brick wall of Heavenly's and watched the door. Considering the commotion on Commercial Street, there was little foot traffic in the alley. Marco fingered the dildo in his pocket. Pop had, of course, refused to put the dildo on display at the jumble sale. He and Aunt Viddie were, for the moment, not on speaking terms as a result of this refusal. I knew, from long experience, that this condition was a temporary one. Sooner or later, one would forget they weren't to speak to the other. I wished that all conflict were that easy to resolve, but I feared that Angelo would not soon forget about Marco, or vice-versa.

I glanced at my watch; in twenty minutes or so, the procession would have found its way to the wharf. Soon after that, people would board their boats for the blessing. The statue of St. Peter would be hoisted ceremoniously to the bow of the *Two Sons*. The entire family, except for Billy, who was captaining the *P-town Queen* for Jeremy, was to be on the boat for the parade.

"We're going to miss the blessing," I said to Marco.

"I'm sorry," said Marco, "but I'd be a sitting duck out on the deck of a boat. You go ahead if you want."

"I'm not so sure you're any safer here," I said, as the door to Heavenly's opened and Angelo strolled into the alley holding a soft drink cup. I knew he was a hit man. A member of the mob capable of God only knew what, but in point of fact, he looked kind of goofy sipping from the straw. In point of fact, we were literally up against a wall with nowhere to go so it was probably a good thing that he didn't look particularly dangerous.

"Go," Marco said, and we crept along the wall trying to get behind him. The ploy didn't work. Angelo looked right at us, smiled, and began moving in our direction. "Marco Tornetti," he said. "Long time no see."

Angelo stepped close enough for us to smell the onions on his breath. Marco thrust the pocketed dildo into Angelo's ribs. Angelo raised his arms, the soda in one hand, into the air. "Mind if I finish my drink?" he said.

"Keep your hands where I can see them," Marco said.

Angelo brought his arms down slowly and took an exaggerated sip of soda. "I don't think you understand the situation we got here," he said.

Chapter Fifty Two

Marco

I understood the situation fine. I understood that, unless I did something, I was going to end up as chum. Angelo put his hand to his jacket. I was pretty sure that the bulge underneath wasn't a dildo. I stuck my pocket with the dildo into his ribs.

I must have been pretty panicked, because I struck him pretty hard. Hard enough that I triggered the switch and the dildo started jiggling around like a go-go dancer. Then, as if that wasn't good enough, Nik and I got to find out why this particular model was called the Bolero. Seemed it had a music chip inside and when you flipped the switch it started to play. "Bolero". Even Angelo was stunned. "What kind of piece you got that plays music and dances?" he asked.

I had nothing but some bravado left so I stuck him again. "You got a problem with my piece?" I said.

Angelo wasn't nearly so dumb as he looked. He gripped the wrist of my hand, the one trying to turn the dildo off, and jerked it from the pocket. I dropped the dildo. It turned circles on the brick walkway. Angelo picked it up and examined it before switching it off and pocketing it. "I got to tell you," he said, "you had me fooled there for a second."

I figured I might as well say my prayers and hope that my Nona had been right about heaven and that she'd put in the good word for me. I raised my hands and was about to tell Angelo he'd won when Nik kneed him. Hard. Right where it hurts. One minute, I'm a goner and the next, Angelo's rolling around on the ground holding his crotch like it's going to fall off.

"Let's get out of here," said Nik, gripping my arm. If there's one thing I knew, it was that I didn't want a hit man after me. Especially if the hit man was upset about taking a knee to the groin.

"We got to stash him somewhere," I said.

"What we've got to do is call the cops. Which is what we should have done in the first place."

"Calling the cops won't help. Phil will just send someone else. We got to come up with a better idea. And we got to stash him someplace while we do that."

Angelo was on all fours, trying to get to his feet. Nikki threatened to kick him again while I snatched the gun from his holster. "Don't move," I said, pointing the weapon at him.

My brain raced like the Indianapolis 500, flipping through all the possible options. And I finally hit on it. The whole town was down at the wharf getting ready for the boat parade and the blessing. Which meant the rest of town was deserted. Jeremy had winked about having something extra-special in mind for the *Queen* and had moored her down at Rusty's marina so as not to spoil the surprise.

Rusty, who had had a brand new dock put in with the insurance money he'd collected, was happy to do it because Jeremy was also talking about selling the boat and using Rusty to broker the sale. If you knocked down the wall of Heavenly Hamburgers, you'd practically be standing in Rusty's showroom.

"Is there a back way to Rusty's from here?" I asked Nikki. I explained my plan. Just so happened there was this galleria across the alley from Heavenly's. And at the back of the galleria was a deck overlooking the harbor. And from the deck you could get to the beach and from the beach you could walk over to the marina.

"I don't like boats," Angelo said.

"Nobody asked you," I said. I gave him a poke with the gun.

"You're not going to use that," said Angelo. To which Nikki raised a knee. Which was enough to get Angelo through the galleria.

I put the gun in my pocket just in case of passersby, but the little galleria was pretty much deserted. I kept the gun poked into Angelo's back in case he got any funny ideas. The *Queen* was sitting pretty as you please in a slip at Rusty's new dock, all decked out in shiny green beads. The plank was down, waiting for Billy and Jeremy to board.

"Jesus and Mary." Angelo stopped dead at the plank. "I can't get on that tub." I poked him with the gun. "You got' it wrong. I'm with..."

"Shut up and move," I said.

"I got this phobia. I don't like boats. I had this dream about drowning in the ocean."

"You don't got a choice," I said.

Nik and I nearly had to drag him up the plank, with Nik threatening to knee him again. We got him below decks; Nik pointed to the ceiling. "Handcuffs?" Angelo asked.

"It's a pleasure cruiser," Nik said, as I fastened the cuffs around his wrists.

"You don't want your dreams to come true, you call Phil right now and tell him the job's done," I said.

"That's what I've been trying to tell you. I don't work for Phil. If you'd let me get a word in without a kick to the boys. I'm with the feds."

"You lie," I said. Angelo might not have been the sharpest tool in the shed, but he was in a jam and he'd say about anything to get out of it.

"I'll prove it to you," he said. "Get my wallet." Nikki reached around and pulled the wallet from his back pocket. Made it look like she was pulling dog crap off a shoe, but she did it.

"Take out the driver's license," Angelo said. "See that number on the back. Call it."

Turned out that Angelo Del Rossi didn't lie. Either that or Fat Phil had set up one hell of a con. "An agent?" I said. I wasn't quite ready to join the faithful.

"Been undercover going on a year and a half, trying to get the goods on Lezario and his goons. Man's been Teflon, but we got a pretty good case with Vlad and the Roma's arson."

"You burned Roma's?"

"Phil's goons burned Roma's. I followed you to the bus station."

"You followed me?"

"When you up and ran. Lucky for me, because I had an excuse not to kill you and to chase a prime witness. You testify and we lock Phil away without the key."

"Don't witnesses end up in the river?" Nikki looked so concerned I could have kissed her right there.

"We'll put him in the witness protection program," Angelo said.

"Couldn't he just stay here? He's already using an alias."

"True that, but Phil knows where he is, so the gig's up."

"Want to quit talking about me like I'm not here?" I got to admit, I was getting a bug up my drawers from all this talk. "I'll decide if I stay or not. It's my neck that's on the block."

"We'll find you a safe place. We do a pretty good job, despite what the papers say."

"And if I don't testify?"

"We take you in on aiding and abetting. And you thank us for sending you up, because if Phil walks you are shark bait."

"Then he testifies. He goes," Nik said.

"What if I don't want to go?"

"It's not like he's family," Nikki said. "He's just some guy that worked for me for a while." I couldn't believe I what I was hearing, but I noticed Nik wouldn't look me in the eye, wouldn't look at me at all. Wasn't even talking to me.

So I called her bluff. "I'm not doing it."

"Yes, you are," she said. "You're going."

Nik could be stubborn. Jesus and Mary, stubborn didn't begin to describe what that woman could be. But I could be stubborn too. I knew damned well what it was she was doing. She was trying to save my life. But my life wasn't worth a steaming pile without Nikki. I was about to say as much when we heard talking up on deck and Jeremy came bounding down the stairs. He stopped dead at the sight of us.

Chapter Fifty Three

Nikki

Jeremy's eyes looked like they were about to pop right out of his head. It took me a second to figure out why, then I noticed that Marco still had Angelo's gun. Angelo took the same second to figure it. "Can you please get me down from here?"

"Don't you do it," Jeremy said. "You've got him right where you want him."

"Everything okay?" Billy's voice came down the stairs from the deck above.

"Fine, honey. Everything's just ducky. You go ahead and get us queued for that parade."

"You sure? You sound a little funny."

"Excited, sweetheart. I'm excited. This whole day has got my adrenaline working overtime."

"Parade?" asked Angelo, as we heard Billy's footsteps move away from the stairs. "This boat?"

Seemed that Angelo had, in the heat of discussion, forgotten he was on a boat. I uncuffed him and he crawled over to the couch and combed his hands through his bristled head. "Parade means leave the dock," he said, sounding nearly as pale as he looked.

"What's wrong with him?" Jeremy asked.

"He's got this phobia," I explained. "Something about a dream and drowning."

"So you bring him aboard the *Queen* knowing he'll be wetting his britches. That is a brilliant plan. The two of you are like Starsky and Hutch, like Cagney and Lacey. Like..."

"Please stop," I said, putting both hands to Jeremy's shoulders. If he'd paced any harder he would have dug a hole in the bottom of the boat.

"He's a cop," Marco handed Angelo his gun.

The engine began to rumble. "I'm going to be sick." Angelo put his head between his legs.

"A cop?" Jeremy looked nearly as pale as Angelo.

"Undercover," said Marco. "FBI"

Billy started the engine, a jarring sound that made Angelo sit up.

"You're a cop?" Jeremy sat next to Angelo.

"We're moving," Angelo said. "Moving out into the open water. Holy mother of God, it's just like in *The Perfect Storm*."

"We're only going out a few hundred yards," I said. "And the harbor's so calm you could skate on it."

"It's just like in my dream. Jesus and Mary, we're all going to drown."

"Nobody's going to drown," I said, as Jeremy jumped up. He took several boxes from under the stairs and moved them into the storage closet in the kitchen. "What are you doing?"

"Forgot to put these away," Jeremy said. "Just tidying. You know me, tidy, tidy, tidy."

I walked over as he put the boxes down. "Atlas," I read before Jeremy gave me a look that might explode.

"Cleaning supplies," Jeremy said. The box read 'fireworks' which explained Jeremy's sudden compulsion to tidy up. Fireworks were illegal in Massachusetts. Though, given the fact that Angelo was breathing as though he were in a Lamaze class while Marco tried to talk him out of the notion of drowning, I doubt that fireworks would have caused Angelo much concern.

"What was that?" Angelo's head came up again, his eyes like Armageddon.

"Billy's turning the boat," I said. "It's fine."

"It's not fine. We're all gonna die."

"No. No. No," said Jeremy. "What you need to do is get your mind off this drowning business. Think happy thoughts."

"Happy thoughts," Angelo looked like he'd be happy to slap the happy thoughts out of Jeremy.

"I know," Jeremy said. He came back with a box from galley storage. "Pop tarts!" he said. "Pop tarts always make me feel better."

"Pop tarts?" I asked.

"I thought you were a gourmet," Marco said.

"Pop tarts are my dirty little secret. You can't eat a pop tart and not smile about it."

"Jesus," said Angelo.

"Strawberry. Yum," said Jeremy, waltzing over to the toaster and popping down two tarts.

Chapter Fifty Four

Marco

We were cruising along real slow, moving out towards the end of the harbor. Jeremy kept going on about pop tarts and happy thoughts. Angelo kept insisting we were all going to die. Funny thing is, the pop tarts were what almost caused us all to die, and it was the slow cruise that saved us.

The toaster that Jeremy put the tarts in was one of those retro popups. Jeremy had bought it from Nick at the flea market. Nick got it on late night TV. The toaster had never been used. Which is why we didn't know about the malfunction. The toaster toasted just fine. It was the popping up that caused the problem.

So there we were, Angelo moaning about what a horrible death drowning is, and me and Nikki trying to tell him that nobody was going to drown, and Jeremy singing "It's a Small World After All" because it was the happiest song he could think of, when we heard a whoosh. The toaster had turned into a flame thrower, the pop tarts exploded into an inferno.

Nikki asked Jeremy where the fire extinguisher was and Jeremy looked at her like he had no idea what a fire extinguisher was. "The fire extinguisher," said Nikki, "for the fire in the galley."

"What fire?" Angelo had yet to discover the flames, being as his head was on his lap with his hands covering it. The word fire made his head pop up like a pop tart.

"Little toaster mishap, not a thing to worry about," said Jeremy, as the three of us played Huckle Buckle Beanstalk looking for the extinguisher. I found it next to the toilet.

"The head?" asked Nikki. "What, in case of shower fires?" She grabbed the canister from me. By that time, though, the paper towels next to the toaster had caught, which had lit up the dishtowel next to the paper towels, which had lit up the pop tart box on the counter. We sprayed a few shots of extinguisher fluid. The fire hissed at us and went right on burning. "It's no use. We have to evacuate," Nikki said.

"What? Leave the boat?" Jeremy asked.

"Hail Mary, full of grace." Angelo was kneeling on the bottom step. Nik and I each grabbed one of his arms. Jeremy was behind us still wondering if it was necessary to evacuate. Nikki ran to the pilot house to tell Billy while I fished out the lifejackets for everyone. I tossed one to Jeremy and helped Angelo put his on. By the time Billy radioed the Coast Guard, there was smoke billowing up the stairs. Nik handed Bill a jacket and put one on herself.

"It's going to take the Guard at least twenty minutes to get here, what with all the boat traffic," Billy said.

Nikki eyed the outermost dock of Rusty's Marina, some five hundred yards across the water. "Think we can make that?" she asked.

"Hell, yes," Billy said.

Nikki turned to us. "We're going to swim to the marina."

"Swim?" Angelo's knuckles were white on the rail. "I can't swim."

"The jacket will keep you afloat," said Billy, taking off his shoes. "It's not that far." Billy climbed over the rail and dove into the water. Nikki, Jeremy, and I also pulled off our shoes, preparing to follow Billy. Angelo eyed the water like it might up and bite him.

"It's easier if you take off your shoes," said Nikki, as Jeremy climbed over the rail, held his nose, and jumped.

Angelo watched him splash in. "I think I'll take my chances with the boat."

"No, you won't," Nikki kneeled and pulled his shoes off. "You either climb up on that rail or Marco and I hoist you over the edge."

Angelo was a big guy and I was pretty sure that Nik and I couldn't hoist him over anything. Angelo called her bluff. "I'll put my knee to your balls and you can die on the ship while holding them," said Nikki, with a look that could make about anyone jump.

"Jesus, lady. You don't have to be such a hard ass." But Angelo had climbed the rail. He sat straddling it. "That's it. I can't do it. I don't want to die like this."

"You'll be fine," said Nik. "Marco and I will help you." She pointed at Billy, who had climbed up onto the dock and was helping Jeremy to do the same.

"I can't do it. I just can't."

We heard a hiss and a pop.

"You don't have a choice," I said. I looked to Nikki. "On three." We gave Angelo a huge shove and sent him flying off the rails and splashing in the water. Nikki and I dove in after him. We each grasped a flailing arm and began towing him towards the dock. It took all four of us to haul the big guy out of the water.

"Oh my holy Fourth of July," said Jeremy. Because the boat looked like she was spewing fire.

"Run!" said Billy. Though he didn't really need to say it. All of us, Angelo included, were already sprinting towards the shore and higher ground. The boat fired and spewed at our backs. We made the street and turned around just in time to see the boat go up in one big grand finale of a display.

Chapter Fifty Five

Parker Bench

The *P-town Queen* made the nightly news: "Big bang at a P-town Festival" was the lead. They interviewed several people standing on McMillan Pier, including one guy who said he thought it was all part of the festivity. The good news was that no one on the pier or in the boat parade was hurt. The bad news was that Rusty's inventory was, for the second time in almost as many months, done in. He had some explaining to do to the insurance guys, but they filed the claim.

Jeremy wasn't so lucky. Fireworks are illegal in the Commonwealth of Massachusetts and the insurance guys weren't willing to pay. Jeremy, in fact, had to pay a three hundred dollar fine for possession. It could have been worse; he could have gone to jail for the display, but Joey Dyer and the other cops took pity on him because he had become a minor celebrity. He and Billy and Nik were all on TV, interviewed for what was called a harrowing escape.

Angelo and I were not on TV, because we weren't officially there. Officially, neither one of us had ever been to Provincetown. Unofficially, Angelo went back to Phil and company with news of my untimely demise in an explosion. He also had a tape of my deposition, which will be used when Phil goes on trial for the murder of Vlad Dostovic next month. And me? I get to stay here forever if I want. As Parker Bench. If I'd known the name change was going to be permanent, I'd have chosen a better name. But, still and all, I'm pretty happy with the deal. I've been working at Ella's as a short-order cook and, maybe by next spring, Billy and Jeremy will have enough investors to finish restoring the Red Tomato. I can see it: checkered table cloths, strolling musicians, and a wine list from here to California. And me in the kitchen with a full menu, everything from white sauce to clam sauce. Everything except gnocchi.

Even if things don't go as planned, I've still got a room at the Silvas'. I still have Nikki, who has decided to stay in town. There's some new interest in her research, due to all the *P-town Queen* publicity, and NOAA, the National Weather folks of all people, are thinking of funding a study. In the meantime, Nikki's working on a whale-watch boat as a naturalist.

Nikki and I walk on the beach a lot these days. Late in the day when the beach people have all gone home, we walk the tide line and watch the sunset. Yesterday, the sunset was really spectacular, this flaming ball going down in a sea of purple.

"Thank you," Nik said, and I wasn't sure if she was thanking the sky for the spectacle or me.

"Thank you for saving my life," she

said, turning to me. I told her that, if anything, she'd saved my life. I mean, who else would have taken a chance on a homeless guy with an alias?

Nikki gave me one of those exasperated Nikki looks I've come to know and said, "You know what today is?"

"The twenty third of August?" I said.

"Ned's wedding. He and Beverly got married. At sunset." I didn't know what to say to that. Nik took my hand. "A few months ago, I probably would have planned to crash the wedding, instead I'm standing on the beach with you, and what Ned does just doesn't matter anymore. I might actually wish him well."

"I hope he's as happy as I am," I said.

"I didn't blow up the Provincetown Inn," she said. "That's progress, right?"

"You've come a long way," I said.

"A long way," she said, "all the way back home."

Home. I got to say, I liked the sound of the word. I lifted Nik's hand and kissed each of her fingers. Then we turned and walked down the beach. Toward home.

About Annie Hoff

Annie Hoff writes comedy and romance. When she's not huddled over a laptop with her 15th cup of coffee, you're likely to find her off watching a play with her hubby, relaxing while listening to music, or out in the woods taking lots of pictures to support her photography habit.

www.ingramcontent.com/pod-product-compliance
Lightning Source LLC
Chambersburg PA
CBHW011502170626
46812CB00008B/2948